THE FALL ON
CHASM'S CLOSE

THE ILLUMINATION OF BRENTON WILDER

STEVEN SNYDER

Cover design and illustration by
Scott Erwert
www.erwert.com

Edited by
Evelyn Lipnia

Produced by:

FriesenPress
Suite 300 – 852 Fort Street
Victoria, BC, Canada V8W 1H8

www.friesenpress.com

Distributed to the trade by The Ingram Book Company

Table of Contents

I would like to thank:

John Malarkey for his encouragement of my writing,
his early feedback, and his constant friendship.

My daughter Grace for listening, reading, editing with me, and
for crying the first time we came to the end of the book.

Scott Erwert for his skill in interpreting the vision for
the cover and turning it into something great.

My wife Patty for her companionship and unend-
ing support for me through difficult times.

My friends who read early manuscripts and gave me posi-
tive feedback and encouragement to keep going.

John Truby's "The Anatomy Of Story" was foundational to my writing.

On Salient Memories

A sound, a thought, a word –
And suddenly
Salient memories, long dormant
Appear unbidden, unexpected
Slender threads of thought through time
Connecting now to then, us to them
Reviving what? We will not know
'Til pain, or love, or joy, or sorrow
Reawaken

1. The Mountain Club

The cool open air of an early spring evening was welcome relief to Brenton, walking west through the Village. At last, he felt free.

It had been a typical day at the Plant. Cooped up all day in a tiny work area with its heavy, stale air, he had been rude to a supervisor who kept a cloak on; it was suspected that she was responsible for the oppressive air that made bulky clothes feel even heavier. His back cramped as he bent over a workstation making birdcages, a job he had no fondness for. He had forgotten to buy more water, making his wheezing worse through the day, labored breathing serving only to remind him of his inescapable disease.

Back at his little cottage on Leeway Street, Brenton turned from locking the gate at the fence to find that he had left the porch gate open; that irritated him. An edge on a boot got caught in floorboards on the porch, nearly tripping him. Safe inside, when he had kicked off his worn boots and began preparing a meal, he noticed the empty birdcage. While he found and caged the little creature the meal burned, filling the house with smoke. He ate what he could and then, eager to escape the foul air, pulled tattered boots back on, slipped on a forest-green jacket, and escaped into the cool evening. Ragged, drifting clouds reflected the last pale hues of the setting sun in an otherwise colorless sky as he carefully turned the locks on the door, the porch gate, and finally, the gate at the fence.

Brenton was walking to the Mountain Club for a Discussion and fresh drinking water; he was in dire need. He had found just enough at the house to ease his wheezing, freeing his chest and giving him the numbing euphoria that temporarily made everything seem alright.

Tonight's Discussion topic, *Freedom in the Village: A Meditation for Ascending Day*, intrigued him, and Brenton thought the feeling of freedom inspired by the cool air an appropriate prelude. Tomorrow was Ascending Day, and that meant he didn't have to be confined at the Plant. Thinking about that as he walked added to a building sense of release.

The broad tunnel just before the Water Dispensary provided an opportunity for the breeze to express itself, refreshing him as he reached the guardhouse at the gate. The guard was preoccupied.

"Hey!" Brenton said loudly, leaning forward. He was annoyed that the guard had ignored his approach.

The guard was still inattentive as Brenton readied a verbal jab, but the guard looked up just in time to avert the assault.

"OK, OK," he said, reaching for keys. He opened the gate to let Brenton into the Water Dispensary enclosure.

A high brick wall on three sides formed the space, with the gate situated in the center of the wall facing the street. A simple, narrow building with wide, drab fascia boards confronted him. The building jutted out of a monolithic, mountainous structure called Mt. Nabal, after the Village; it was also home to the Mountain Club. Four narrow steps led up to a shallow porch and the attendant's window, allowing only one individual to approach the window at a time, making water procurement a singular but efficient ritual. Brenton stepped up to the iron-barred window.

"I need water." He could barely make out the features of the attendant in the dark beyond the window, but he saw enough, as the attendant's eyes rolled.

"It isn't free, you know," came the response.

"I know that, you..." Brenton bit his lip and finished silently...*idiot.* He checked himself, not wanting trouble with anyone associated with the Mountain Club or the Nutrition Bureau. He slapped the coin he had been reaching for on the counter, flicked it under the bar, and then put his container below an opening in the wall. A chill suddenly took him, and he pulled his jacket tight.

Inside, a lever was pulled and presently a trickle of blue water drained down a spout. The Dispenser delivered a small amount of the liquid, the flow stopping before long. Brenton took a sip to ease his wheezing, and then stomped off the porch, out the gate, and off toward the auditorium inside the mountainous structure, his boots sounding out what his sharp tongue wanted to.

In the foyer, Brenton surveyed the room looking for familiar faces. The small group that Brenton associated with all worked at the Plant, spent holidays together, and climbed together on Ascending Day. They had even lived together for a time under the same roof.

Brenton's forest-green jacket made him stand out in the crowd, and soon a tap on the shoulder had him turning. He saw Mark and Meyer, both regulars at the Mountain Club, as was Joe, whom Brenton had yet to locate. They had been friends for a long time, even though Brenton was typically brisk with them.

"Hey," Brenton managed flatly, still irritated. "Have you seen Joe?"

"He's talking to Father Bayle," offered Mark, nodding toward the auditorium.

"Yeah, you know how Joe likes to rile him up," added Meyer. Then his brow furrowed as he quietly added, "Verdie was even better at it."

At the name, Brenton's thoughts returned to the day when Verdie had left Nabal in a driving rainstorm. Father Bayle had tried to dissuade her, but in the end she left amid his protests. He spat dire warnings about the dangers that lay ahead of her, and after she left, sounding like a bitter, disappointed parent, Father Bayle dismissed her as a strong-minded fool who would come to no good. Brenton didn't know where she had gone, and he missed her.

"Let's find a seat," Mark suggested.

They entered the auditorium and spotted Joe and Father Bayle near the platform in animated dialogue. Now it was time for the Discussion, and Father Bayle patted Joe on the back, dismissing him. The friends waved as he turned, and soon the four were seated together.

"What was that about?" Meyer asked.

Joe chuckled. "The usual conversation," he said smiling, eyes fixed on the figure mounting the stage; he didn't need to say more.

Joe was an energetic skeptic, and brighter than most Villagers. He and Father Bayle disagreed on many subjects, and Joe took great pleasure in often spurring debate. Joe greeted Brenton—he always had a kind word, even when Brenton was cold or distant—and then turned toward the speaker.

Father Bayle was at the lectern, smiling broadly, inviting all to find a seat. He relished Discussion evenings and Ascending Days, when everyone in Nabal was expected to attend, as these occasions gave him a captive audience, allowing him to wax eloquent on a variety of very deliberately chosen topics.

"Another 'discussion' is about to begin," Joe muttered under his breath to no one in particular. "I can't wait."

Father Bayle was the Master of the Mountain Club and Headmaster of the school. No one could remember how he came by the title "Father," but that's what everyone called him. No one could even say when he first arrived in the Village, but in many ways, he *was* the Village.

In showing apparent concern for the Villagers, Father Bayle was considered a nice man. He was known around Nabal for his acts of kindness, and had been for as long as anyone could recall. His loyal little dog Yap was almost always by his side, except on these Discussion nights.

Father Bayle wore a red hat with a shallow bowl, broad brim cocked to one side, and a crimson robe with a high, buttoned collar to match the hat. His garb was an anomaly, the combination of dress and color contrasting awkwardly with Nabal's population whose typical attire, provided through the Plant, was dull hues of green, brown and gray. Their trousers were bulky, shirts and blouses heavy and oversized, boots cumbersome and poorly made.

Father Bayle wore high, black boots with a buckle—decidedly not from the Plant—finished with a heel that clicked rhythmically on the hard surfaces of the Village.

"Tonight's topic," Father Bayle began, smiling eyes slowly taking in a rapt audience, "is a subject dear to my person. Let us all meditate on it as we survey our homes, and indeed, our Village, from the mountaintop on the morrow."

By design, Discussions always preceded Ascending Days.

He continued, his script memorized. "Freedom in the Village: A Meditation for Ascending Day." He surveyed the room for a moment, then, "What is freedom?" he asked with a flourish, pausing for dramatic effect. He then listed freedoms that the Villagers enjoyed in a rambling homily which invariably pointed in some way to him. Father Bayle had a way of doing that, and no one seemed to mind, or even notice.

No one, that is, except Joe.

The speaker went on to remind the Villagers that they were free to associate, to congregate and to come and go as they pleased. "There is no lock on the Village gate," he asserted proudly.

Next, the eloquent speaker praised the Nutrition Bureau for their tireless efforts in providing food and drinking water. One day, he believed, the technicians at the Nutrition Bureau would be able to create even better water.

He stopped short of saying anything about healing their diseased bodies. Most Villagers refused to believe that they were sick, sipping the blue water all day, its properties masking their symptoms and pleasantly numbing their minds.

Father Bayle continued by extolling the Banking Bureau for the annual Preservation Reward. On an annual basis the Banking Bureau audited the money and possessions of each person in the Village, awarding them a Preservation Reward based on what they had retained.

He then went on to remind them that their Village was free of crime, they were free to work at the Plant, free to use the Village gardens— most of which were gated, locked and overgrown with thorns, observed Joe quietly—to receive free clothes, and very importantly, they were free to seek Father Bayle's comfort and advice on matters of importance, such as financial concerns or travel.

Applause rang out when he reminded them that tomorrow was Ascending Day, and that the potent drink of water provided for them on the mountaintop was absolutely free. He nodded and smiled, one hand raised palm outward, as the applause died down.

He rambled on for a while, getting sidetracked on personal anecdotes and listing other freedoms that the Villagers enjoyed, then he paused again, looking around the room.

Joe filled the brief silence for his friends with a low, singsong, "Here we go-o." After a lifetime of listening to Father Bayle, he knew how the Discussion would end.

Father Bayle began again, more forcefully now.

"Most importantly you are free from the dangers of that Mountain at the edge of the Flatlands, and the tyranny of those people." His voice was even and stern, his arm and forefinger stretched straight, pointing west toward The Mountain.

He never named the people that lived there.

"Your ancestors tried assailing it at their peril!" he insisted, as Joe rolled his eyes. Father Bayle's voice had risen to a crescendo, and then trailed off. He continued quietly, just above a whisper, his index finger now tapping the lectern. "But here, right here in the Village, the Mountain Club has provided for you, free of charge," —now his voice was rising again, with his arm— "your very own mountain, that you can triumphantly climb each Ascending Day,"—and here he pointed upward towards the unseen mountaintop on the structure far above him, his outstretched arm pumping the air, and he nearly shouted—"so that you can say 'I have been to the mountaintop!' and you can really mean it..." —then trailing off in a near-whisper— "really mean it." He bit his lower lip, eyes closed, slightly bowed head bobbing slowly from side to side.

The dramatics elicited applause from the audience. All, that is, except Joe—and for the first time Brenton held still following the inevitably dramatic conclusion of another Discussion. At the reference to ancestors in that final monologue, something snagged in Brenton's mind, tearing at subtle silken threads, carefully woven, binding faint memory. For a moment he saw his mother—and storybooks—their colorful pictures etched indelibly somewhere in dim recesses. A long-ago feeling flashed through his mind ever so briefly, then died away.

As he gazed over the room taking in the accolades, the keen eye of Father Bayle landed on Brenton and Joe, taking note of their lack of enthusiasm for his Discussion. When the clapping ended, he closed by reminding everyone about Ascending Day, thanked them for coming and dismissed them with a wish for a good evening. As the congregation rose to depart, he briskly descended the steps and purposefully made his way to a small knot of men wearing the field-grey uniform of the Nutrition Bureau, distinct with high collared shirt.

Joe had noticed Brenton's tranquil response to the speech, while Mark and Meyer were oblivious. The friends rose silently to leave, making their way out into the cool evening, parting in twos.

Joe and Brenton walked dim avenues in subtle moonlight until Joe finally broke the silence.

"What were you thinking back there?"

"I can't say for sure," responded Brenton, and they walked for a time before he chose to continue. "Something Father Bayle said about ancestors brought up an old memory, and whatever it was, for just a moment it set my mind thinking of my mother and storybooks. At the end, I didn't want to clap. That's all I know."

Joe nodded knowingly, and without speaking took his thoughts with him as they parted for the evening.

Brenton arrived back at his house and got a boot stuck on the porch again. Inside, he made sure that the bird was still in its cage, then poured blue drinking water, draining a cup. Immediately his breathing eased, he felt the euphoria he craved, and the memory of how the Discussion had ended faded away in mind-numbing bliss.

Under a pale moon, a solitary figure in field-grey stepped out of shadow and down the deserted street, while a second form, close-cloaked and hooded, slipped silently out of concealment and inched cautiously, deliberately, toward the little cottage on Leeway Street.

On The Nature Of "Real"

Fraying threads, life's tapestry
Might one day fade to shadow
When grander Truth comes into view
An unimaginable future
Rendering the real—so-called
A fleeting thought
An unattainable memory

2. An Invitation to Climb

Brenton slept well, waking as he often did to the sound of his captive little bird. He rose anticipating a day to himself, even if he did have to spend some of it climbing Mt. Nabal. He unlocked the front door, stepping onto the porch to take in the morning sun, shining pale through still, heavy air. He yawned and stretched, face upraised, skin grasping for warmth, eyes closed. He lowered his head and shook away clinging sleep-cobwebs, and as he opened his eyes they fell on a little parcel by the porch gate. He dropped to one knee and noticed the letter "B" written neatly in one corner. He looked around, scooped up his find and slipped back inside, clicking locks.

The package was flat with a crude, dark twine holding the contents securely. Brenton cut the twine and carefully unwrapped the folded packet, finding a little piece of rough paper. His eye was drawn to a little image on the top left corner—a triad of overlapping pickaxes. He had seen the emblem before, and though straining to remember where, he turned his attention to the little poem on the paper, reading it aloud:

> The real you sense
> Is surely not
> The real that Real
> Can be
> If you would taste
> The really Real
> I urge you, Climb with me!

He read it several times. *Well, it is Ascending Day after all, but I've never been invited to climb before,* he thought. Bells would ring out the Invitation to Climb, and there was the invitation that Father Bayle always issued, a ceremony inviting everyone to climb Mt. Nabal just before the event, but these were for everyone. Brenton turned the paper over, finding another puzzle:

On Ascending Day, drink only clear water

Brenton thought for a moment. *Father Bayle does administer water at the top of Mt. Nabal—it's definitely stronger than the water from the Dispensary, but it's also just as blue. What does "clear water" mean?* At the bottom of the paper there was a less cryptic sentence:

Come visit me! V

He remembered the mention of Verdie the night before; she used to call him "B," and he called her "V." He turned the paper over again and looked at the overlapping pickaxes. *That's definitely a climbing tool,* he thought, *but there's nothing about a pickaxe associated with the Mountain Club.*

A vague idea began to form, and he looked out the window in the direction of The Mountain, dim and hazy on the edge of the Flatlands, its peak perpetually hidden in clouds. Father Bayle often warned Brenton and his friends about its dangers; every Discussion night ended with rantings against The Mountain and an exhortation to satisfy the Flatlander's inherent desire to climb with a trip up Mt. Nabal on Ascending Day. Brenton thought about Verdie and her last encounter with Father Bayle, wondering what he might know about her whereabouts.

The idea that this was indeed a note from Verdie began to take hold, with its clear invitation to visit and a reference to climbing, although Brenton didn't understand the use of the word "Real." If it was from Verdie, he couldn't take it to his former mentor to learn more, knowing how Father Bayle felt about her. Brenton cared enough for memories of her that he didn't want them sullied by a verbal assault. *Besides,* he thought, *Joe and I haven't visited Father Bayle for a long time.*

The thought of Joe gave Brenton the idea that he might help unravel clues, but if he were to ask questions he had to hurry, as the bells that signaled the Invitation to Climb would be pealing soon. He gobbled some food, got dressed, and pulled on deteriorating boots. He threw on his forest-green jacket, tucked the small parcel into his pocket, grabbed his climbing pack, and hurried out the door, locking down the house and gates.

As he turned from locking the gate at the fence, he was ready to hurry off down the street when he was interrupted abruptly by his neighbor, Mr. Parish, blocking his way. He was wearing slippers and a robe and he wheezed heavily, holding a flask. Mr. Parish had difficulty walking and often asked Brenton to buy water for him; Brenton would begrudgingly agree if he couldn't make an excuse. When Mr. Parish was desperate, he would ask to borrow water.

"Could...uhh...I...uhh...get...uhh...some...uhh...water...uhh...son," he wheezed painfully.

Even when he wasn't in a hurry Brenton found Mr. Parish annoying.

"Can't help," Brenton blurted, brushing past the old man, nearly knocking him into the ditch. Parish was left wheezing on the walkway.

Joe's house was a short distance away, and soon Brenton was banging on a locked gate. Joe appeared, confused, asking, "Did I miss the Invitation to Climb?" thinking that Brenton's urgency was related to Ascending Day.

"No, but I have an invitation to climb with me." That brought Joe up short at the gate with an inquisitive look.

Had he not been so focused on Brenton as he crossed the porch, he might have seen the little package wrapped in crude twine lying next to the porch gate, with a neat little "J" written in one corner.

Inside the house Joe looked over Brenton's curious packet.

"I know that symbol," Joe said without hesitation. "This is an invitation to climb The Mountain, and that pickaxe cluster means it's from a Helper."

Brenton was curious, saving questions, and then he remembered where he had seen the pickaxe. They turned their attention to the other side of the paper, Brenton addressing the "V."

"Could it be Verdie?" he asked, pointing.

Joe smiled at him, a hand on his shoulder.

"Do you know any other Helpers with a name starting with "V" who want you, "B," to visit them?"

Brenton knew little about the people at The Mountain whom Father Bayle wouldn't name. Brenton had seen them in the Village occasionally, with their light, bright clothing, and their unusual shoes, both men and women with long-handled pickaxes strapped to their backs. The dawning idea that Verdie had gone to The Mountain and may have even become a Helper sent Brenton into momentary silence; then, gathering his thoughts he focused on the pressing issue of the water.

"On Ascending Day, drink only clear water," Joe read aloud; his mouth spread in a broad grin. "I knew it!" he shouted excitedly, grabbing Brenton by the shoulders, shaking him. "Brenton, do you even begin to understand what this means?"

"No, that's why I came over!" Brenton shot back.

Joe tried to calm down and went on.

"Ok, follow along: If this *is* from a Helper—which it must be—and if it *is* from Verdie—which it also must be—then she's sending you a warning!"

"About Ascending Day?" Brenton looked puzzled.

"No! About the water that Father Bayle gives the climbers at the top of the mountain. Verdie is telling us that there's something about the water, and the use of the word "real" in the first poem makes me think something isn't real, or there is something more real than we know."

Although he was in his own house, Joe looked around as if someone or something could be eavesdropping, then went on.

"Can I tell you something that you must never tell anyone?"

"Joe, we practically grew up together. You can trust me!"

Joe smiled and patted Brenton's shoulder, his nervous excitement palpable.

"I've been doing some experimenting on myself," Joe began. "On days when we don't have to be at the Plant, I don't drink the water from the Water Dispensary."

"What?" Brenton's face twisted, and he started to say more.

"Hold on for the rest." Joe's palm was up. "Yes, my symptoms get really bad, but I've been able to stand it long enough to discover something." Brenton was both calm and curious as Joe continued. "I think much more clearly and quickly when I haven't had any water...I get flashes of memory, like the one you had last night."

Brenton hesitated as he thought for a moment, remembering that he hadn't had his normal ration of water the day before.

"What does it mean?" he asked, a strange uneasiness beginning to grow.

"Well, I can't prove anything conclusively, but I have a growing suspicion that the water from the Dispensary has something in it—an additive—something that dulls your mind, and at the same time masks the disease and makes you feel good."

Brenton was skeptical, though he knew the disease was real. He liked the water. It gave him a pleasurable sensation and staved off his symptoms; it was necessary. There was only one source of water in the Village, and one reason that the people of Nabal rarely traveled was the old adage drilled into them from childhood: stay near the source.

"What does your experimenting have to do with Ascending Day water?" Brenton asked, struggling for a connection.

Joe was excited as he went on.

"Our daily water and Ascending Day water are both cloudy blue. A friend outside the Village is telling us to drink clear water, and hinting at something more real than we know of."

Brenton thought about Joe's logic for a moment.

"I've never seen clear water, so I wouldn't know where to find some to drink," Brenton said flatly.

Joe's suspicions were finding footing in his own mind, and now he began to suggest ideas that Brenton had never considered.

"Where is the Water Dispensary located, and who dispenses the water at the top of Mt. Nabal on Ascending Day?"

Brenton fell silent at the implication of Joe's suggestion; he didn't want Joe to continue. He didn't want trouble with anyone, and he didn't want to hear even the suggestion that things weren't as they seemed, or that something was in the water. He was comfortable, content with things just as they were. The Village was his home, he had everything he needed, and he just wanted things to remain the same. He wanted to protect what he had, collect his annual Preservation Reward, and keep to himself—and he didn't want to believe anything suspicious about Father Bayle.

"I think you're going too far, Joe." Brenton's tone was even and cold, sounding a vague warning.

Joe's response was quick.

"I'm just looking at the facts, and I've been thinking for a long time, more and more often without the foggy head I get when I drink Dispensary water."

Joe wasn't confrontational; he was just thinking farther and faster than Brenton, and he knew that it would take time for the thought that he had planted in Brenton's mind to germinate and grow into belief. Brenton's ideas about truth would have to crumble before new ideas could take hold.

Brenton wasn't sure how to proceed, and he didn't want to take the discussion further, or argue with...

Bells shattered the silence and with it the tension in the room. Immediately a shared purpose imposed its will on the friends, returning thoughts to companionship.

"We should go." Brenton exhaled the words, relieved at the distraction.

Joe took a flask from the kitchen, grabbed his climbing pack and opened the door, letting Brenton out. He turned to lock the door while Brenton faced the street.

"Joe!" Brenton exclaimed, pointing down. Joe stooped and picked up a small package, noticing the letter "J'" and then broke the twine and opened it. The note inside, written on crude paper, was identical to Brenton's. Joe showed it to him, smiled as he pocketed it, and together the friends responded to the Invitation to Climb.

Behind them a lithe figure, grey hood pulled low, walked quickly south and west along back avenues and quiet paths through the Village, and with no one around to notice, slipped out the Village gate.

3. Ascending Day

Brenton and Joe walked quickly, silently toward the Mountain Club. Thin clouds filtered warmth and deflected pale sunlight, making objects appear flat and lifeless. Like bees swarming toward a hive, Villagers were on the move, a single thought throbbing, drumming in their collective mind.

The companions passed through the tunnel near the Water Dispensary, then angled for the landing where the climbing ramp found connection to the Village floor. Brenton and Joe found Mark and Meyer, and the friends stood talking on the pavement as Villagers flocked around them. Father Bayle could be seen moving through the congregating crowd, meeting and greeting even as he forged toward the ramp, acting out the image of the Village's benevolent mentor and leader. Yap, collared and crimson leashed, followed obediently.

Near the friends a small group was protesting the climb, chanting about mountains. Brenton recognized their clothing which identified them as Climbers, another group who lived at The Mountain. Father Bayle tolerated them although he wasted no time talking about them. Many Climbers kept homes in the Village, and they were at Mt. Nabal every Ascending Day and often protested at the Village Bureaus.

Before long, several representatives from the Nutrition Bureau in distinct field-grey moved the group slowly, and with little commotion, away from the gathering crowd, whose minds were set on the climb and the reward that awaited them; they paid no attention to the Climbers.

Presently the bells rang again, and stillness fell over the congregants as every soul turned toward the figure that would lead the procession. Father Bayle, positioned slightly up the ramp, raised a hand to silence the already stilled crowd; he loved ceremony, and he adored being central to it.

"Friends and companions," he began in an overly dramatic affectation, "I greet you on this fine Ascending Day. Come, come and share with me in this adventure, this climb to the mountaintop!" His voice rose as he reached the end of the familiar sentence. His arm was extended, and he pointed triumphantly toward the peak of the structure. Joe, in the middle of the group of friends, raised his hands in mockery, elbows close to his sides, and like a symphony conductor, prepared for a dramatic downbeat that he would match to the tired words he knew were coming.

As if on cue, Father Bayle stretched out his arms, welcoming in the whole assembly, and in a loud voice shouted out, "I bid you, come and climb with me!" The invitation was officially extended, with its typical pomp and empty ceremony, and Joe's extended hands fell and then rose slightly outward in a curl at the perfectly synchronous moment. He smiled at his own antics.

Brenton's thoughts were dominated by the morning's events, and now he was fixated on the awkwardly clad figure on the ramp, seeing Father Bayle through a filter imposed by uninvited thoughts that he rebelled against at the core of his being. He had no problem with Father Bayle, and the two of them had a long history though many memories had faded. But now, building on the flash of memory from the night before, the notes from Verdie and the conversation with Joe, doubt crept inexorably across the threshold of his mind like a nefarious imp, gaining ground as it strained forward, crawling against his will, crowding into the very chamber of ideas that he held true. The packet, its contents, the discussion that ensued, Joe's deductions, his secret, the implications— all of it churned in Brenton's mind, as all around him the Villagers moved like driven cattle toward the ramp, the four friends moving with the crowd, their own wills subsumed by the overwhelming will of the crowd to climb—a pressing, crushing will that none of them could resist, moving them all towards the inevitable. At the head of the procession Father Bayle, clutching his furry, tethered possession, began the walk up the winding ramp, beckoning the assembly with broad, empty gestures; he was the Grand Marshall of his very own parade.

The ramp clung to Mt. Nabal like a constrictor to its victim, and ended at a platform that constituted the mountaintop that Father Bayle had spoken about so passionately in his Discussion. Today, as on every Ascending Day, the Villagers would find relief from the climb in the water that Father Bayle would administer. The water on Ascending Day was more potent than daily water, and it both quelled the dizziness from the height, which the Health Bureau claimed was a Flatlander trait, and provided pleasurable sensations that relaxed the mind. The pleasant effect of the water was the main reason that all of Nabal turned out each Ascending Day, willingly following Father Bayle and submitting to his ceremonies.

The friends weren't far up the winding ramp before Joe provided commentary on their journey. "Quite a trek!" he said with mock wheezing, everything about him dripping sarcasm.

Joe challenged his world. Somewhere, deep inside, he heard a quiet whisper telling him that things around him were not what they seemed. He longed for a companion to travel with him down roads of possibility and discovery. The little package had fueled that desire, and now he was as determined as ever to pursue the Real that the little poem alluded to. He believed that Brenton would be that trusted companion on the road into the unknown, and now he had shared intimately and trusted that Brenton would keep those secret thoughts safe.

His thoughts now turned to the ceremony at the top, and he had a decision to make. He broached the subject with his climbing partner. "Are you going to drink the water?" he whispered in Brenton's ear.

Brenton was lost in thought, but Joe's words mirrored them.

"I don't think so," he said hesitantly. He was not as convinced as Joe about the water, but like pieces of a puzzle, various thoughts and dim memories of incidents past were coalescing into a picture in his mind. He wheezed heavily, not from the climb, which was little more than an upwardly angled walk, but because in the urgency to get the package to Joe before the bells rang out, he had neglected to drink any water, making his mind clearer than usual; he was becoming more aware.

"How will we avoid drinking it?" Brenton asked.

Joe was already thinking about the mountaintop, Father Bayle, and his method for administering the water.

For his Ascending Day ceremony, Father Bayle stood behind a draped table on a small dais at one end of the flat mountaintop. A low wall surrounded the space, and here and there large, cracked pots filled with dry dirt, and what was left of long-dead plants, were situated. Villagers approached the dais in single file, climbed the steps, and received a small cup of the potent, blue liquid. They were expected to drink, cross the dais, discard the cup into a bin, and go down the steps on the other side where they would file around the edge of the space, allowing them to look down on the Plant, the Bureaus, and their homes, as Father Bayle had instructed the night before.

Mt. Nabal was in the very center of the circular, walled Village, and as they filed around the space, the climbers could look over the landscape in every direction, with a bird's eye view of the Bureaus situated around the Mountain Club, the Plant, and beyond these buildings, their own little cottages. Eight main roads spread out in every direction from the center, and a web of connecting roads and paths encircled Mt. Nabal. Beyond the Village walls lay the barren Flatlands, without streams or rivers in their broad expanse, their absence reinforcing the oft-repeated advice to stay near the source.

The only unnatural feature visible in the Flatlands was the huge ranch with pasture, crops and flower fields situated at a crossroads about a day's walk from Nabal. Managed by the Nutrition Bureau, it was the source of food and water for the Village. On the horizon, on the far edge of the Flatlands and beyond a series of barely visible large water tanks and storage buildings on the ranch, loomed the cloud-topped Mountain, dim in the pale light and surrounded by a lake, like a moat around a fortress. Father Bayle could do nothing to keep the climbers from taking in the sight of The Mountain; he could only warn them about its many dangers and provide a safe alternative.

As they rose above the Village, the climbers looked down on the wagons from the Nutrition Bureau, which were parked in a gated enclosure on the opposite side of the mountain from the Water Dispensary. A large, guarded door allowed the wagons' entry into the belly of the mountain; they were the source of the daily drinking water that Villagers required. On most days, the Nutrition Bureau wagons were on the streets, in various stages of delivery between the Bureau, the Mountain Club, and the Village gate, on their way to the ranch down the road. The workers on the wagons wore field-grey uniforms and kept to themselves, the Nutrition Bureau maintaining dormitories for them both at the ranch and at the Bureau in the Village, insulating them from Village life. After shuffling around the enclosure and taking in all these sights, Villagers were to file back down the mountain to activities below, or back to their little houses.

As the friends walked the ramp, Joe had been developing a plan to trick Father Bayle, and he shared it quietly with Brenton, who tried to visualize the plan for himself, and when he felt that he could pull it off, he nodded, and the two walked on. Behind them, Mark and Meyer saw the exchange, but did not hear what had transpired between the conspirators.

Up and up they climbed, the Village, pale and colorless in the weak sunlight, laid out below them, Brenton's mind racing ahead to part two of the plan: finding clear water. His clearing mind still had no idea what course of action they should take, and his wheezing was getting worse. He noted with curiosity that he was not getting dizzy as he normally would by climbing to this height. Returning to thoughts of clear water, Brenton asked Joe about the culmination of their plan.

"What about the clear water?" he asked.

Joe was thinking ahead too.

"Let's get off the top as fast as we can," Joe whispered. He reasoned that getting down the ramp as far ahead of Father Bayle as possible might give them time to get into the inner workings of the mountain to find something—anything—that would put flesh on the bones of their suspicions. The friends had been near the ramp and the head of the line at the beginning of the climb; if they could get past the Villagers ahead of them on the way down they might be able to make it to the head of the descent, allowing them to gain even more time.

They were at the top now, in line for water, and as they moved closer, Joe thought of Mark and Meyer. Although the four were friends, he didn't trust them like he trusted Brenton, and he had an idea of what he would tell them. Father Bayle loomed just ahead of them on the dais, visible to all on the mountaintop, handing water to each climber in turn, with the ceremony proceeding smoothly as Joe mounted the platform.

Father Bayle smiled and handed Joe a cup, while the little leashed dog sat contentedly next to his master, taking in the spectacle. Joe executed the plan, and Father Bayle's focus was on Brenton as Joe moved past him and quietly spit the water back into the cup and deposited it into the bin. *So far so good*, Joe thought to himself. Father Bayle's focus remained on the approaching climbers; he had no need to keep an eye on everyone himself. Brenton received his portion and knocked it back, nearly choking it down, catching himself, and moving on. He struggled with drinking the water to still his heavy wheezing, doing his best to control his breathing in front of Father Bayle, but safely finished his role. He moved down the stairs and joined Joe at the rim of the mountaintop enclosure, shuffling sideways and facing outward like all the others.

Pleased with their performance, Joe smiled at Brenton as he spoke.

"I'll tell Mark and Meyer that we have a bet on who will get down first."

Brenton nodded.

Mark and Meyer were both smiling as they joined Joe and Brenton at the wall. They were neither wheezing nor dizzy, experiencing the pleasant effects of the liquid. They all shuffled around the mountaintop, pushing past the randomly distributed pots and their unfortunate contents. No one spoke, and Brenton tried to control his wheezing, by now committed to the plan, although uncertainty about Joe's inferences remained. The shuffling friends reached the ramp and started to descend in single file, while all around them the recipients of Father Bayle's offering were feeling its full effects, relaxed in body and mind, providing Joe and Brenton an opportunity to make their move. Joe spoke over his shoulder.

"Brenton and I have a bet on who will get down first," he explained to the relaxed Mark.

"Ok, Joe, that sounds fine." Mark wasn't slurring, but his speech was sluggish, and he slowly repeated the message to Meyer.

The friends were well below the rim and away from Father Bayle's view when Joe and Brenton began gently pushing between the descending Villagers ahead of them on the ramp and the last of the ascending congregation. Seeing that they were approaching the front of the line, they quickened their pace. Brenton had a question that he had to ask Joe.

"Were you dizzy at all up there?"

Concentrating as he had been on the plan, Joe hadn't even thought about what they had always believed was a symptom of their sickness, and he smiled and shook his head.

The ashen sun shone pale through stale air, and almost no one seemed to notice as the two got past the leader of the descent and ran ahead, down the winding ramp, into the unknown.

On The Rebel Heart

The restless rebel heart, unbound
Draws purpose for a course unclear
From wells of truth unseen, yet deep
A yearning for the better
In quiet, filled by whispers soft
From whom, or where, it does not know
Then worlds ignite, to spring anew
When yearning hearts catch fire

4. In the Belly of the Mountain

With the guarded Water Dispensary and water wagon gate out of the question, the only accessible entrance into the mountain was the foyer of the auditorium. The foyer was left open so that Villagers could access a small library containing past Discussions and other writings by Father Bayle, and a kitchen where food was sold through a narrow window after work and Ascending Day climbs. The auditorium was also left open, and Father Bayle kept an office adjoining it, regularly entertaining Villagers who sought help or advice. Connected to the office by a locked door were his generous apartments.

Expecting the foyer to be unlocked, Joe was not disappointed when the door opened, the two adventurers slipping inside alone. Joe had a plan; both wheezed heavily, but Joe had the advantage of his practice at staying away from the temptation of the water, and he was thinking clearly.

"Let's try the office," he suggested, and Brenton had no argument, wanting only to find out whatever they could and get some water, any water; he had never been this dehydrated, and he was suffering. He followed Joe into the auditorium and onto the stage, now very aware that his head had cleared considerably. The plausibility of Joe's assertions was growing on him as Joe tried the handle of the office door, but it was locked.

Brenton's memory was improving with time, and he was very familiar with the Mountain Club; he remembered climbing through the narrow window into the kitchen to sneak food as a youngster.

"The kitchen!" he blurted out.

They both turned and ran down the steps, out of the broad auditorium, heading for the narrow hall with the window at the end. The window was smaller than Brenton remembered, but it was the only possibility of penetrating the structure. First he tried the kitchen door, but it too was locked. They stripped off packs and coats, pushing them through the narrow opening into the kitchen, and then Joe tried to squeeze through.

It was difficult, but he managed by putting his arms inside, grasping the edge of the counter, and then pulling himself in. Brenton followed with difficulty, but Joe was able to help.

Inside the kitchen, they began looking through cupboards, finding loaves, cheese, and serving dishes, but no liquid. Brenton was closest to the small window when he heard movement up the hall, and motioning for silence, listened. He heard talking and the occasional door closing, but no one was near the kitchen. The climbers had descended back to the Village floor and some had simply wandered into the building as they might on any such occasion. Joe and Brenton returned to their task.

There were small, slatted doors along both walls at the back of the kitchen, with a larger door at the end of the room. Brenton recalled that the smaller doors were for storage, and the two soon confirmed that these were indeed pantries. After this discovery, the friends found themselves standing in front of the portal at the end of the room. The door had a lock, but they had no key and no hope of finding one, and they looked at each other before Brenton stepped forward. He grabbed the handle, closed his eyes and pushed down. The handle gave, there was a click, but the door was locked. They were at a dead end. If they couldn't escape the confines of the kitchen, they had little hope of pursuing their plan, vague as it was, and they were discussing what to do next when they heard a noise in the hall. Clunking boots moved toward the kitchen.

Without time to think, Joe opened the nearest pantry door on the right and they scrambled in. A lock turned and the kitchen door opened and closed. Brenton, nearest the pantry door, turned and found that he could barely see out through the slats, so he beckoned Joe. A figure in a field-grey uniform—the Water Dispensary attendant—was walking toward the back door. He entered the pantry opposite their hideout, emerged and approached the door, and they heard the turn of a lock. The man replaced the key somewhere in the pantry, closed it, and walked through the door, turning the bolt inside.

They paused to listen, then cautiously crossed into the opposite storeroom, when they heard the faint sound of a door close inside the mountain. Joe soon found the key high on a shelf, while with his ear to the big door, Brenton listened for any more sounds beyond it. Joe turned the lock, replaced the key, and returned. Now they had to be cautious, using hand signals and nods to communicate. Brenton pushed the handle down and quietly opened the door just enough to peek through, the door opening on to a large, open space.

They could see some large wooden casks on the floor, and a platform with a table on it where smaller containers of different sizes were situated. They looked at one another, each gauging how intrepid the other might be. Brenton tapped his ear, pointing inside the huge room, wanting to proceed, and Joe nodded at the silent suggestion. The pair craned their necks, pressing their ears at the opening into the uncertainties that awaited them, hearing only a sound from overhead.

Everyone climbed Mt. Nabal on Ascending Days, from Father Bayle to the smallest child in the Village, and the muffled sound of lazily marching feet could be heard above them, hundreds of boots scratching out a sound like a bird's wings beating against the sides of a confining box.

No other sound came from the storeroom, so they cautiously proceeded, Brenton entering first, opening the door only as far as was necessary to pass through. Joe quickly followed, very gently shutting the door behind him.

They were in a cavernous room, with rounded walls sloping upward, and they were very exposed as they took in as much of their surroundings as they could in the dim lamplight. To the left, against the inside wall of the mountain, steps led to a platform with two doors, which appeared to be the back of the outward facing Water Dispensary. One door was meant for a person, which they assumed the attendant had just entered, no doubt serving Villagers lined up to get water to take home, their potent Ascending Day water inevitably wearing off. The other door appeared to be for the casks standing in neat rows on the floor, labeled with large black letters: "Nutrition Bureau." Brenton broke the long silence.

"We could hide among those casks if we have to," he whispered, eliciting a nod from Joe.

They had not yet discovered anything new, as the familiar casks were always clearly visible on wagons moving in and out of the Village, and between the Nutrition Bureau and Mt. Nabal. Brenton pointed Joe's attention to the platform in front of them, which adjoined the back wall of a giant box; it was the auditorium inside the cavernous mountain. From the platform a stair climbed to the top of the structure, and atop the auditorium, situated directly below the mountaintop and reaching to it, a narrow, circular stair rose high in a tight spiral. A trap-door was barely visible at the top, and based on its location on the underside of the mountaintop, it appeared to lead to the dais where Father Bayle administered the Ascending Day water. Brenton had never noticed a hatch from the outside, but then he recalled the covered table that Father Bayle used for the water. A rope at the top hung off of pulleys, reaching to the roof of the auditorium.

Their wheezing was worsening as they moved to the large casks.

"Let's open one," Joe suggested as he indicated his choice, and Brenton agreed, finding a pry bar nearby on the platform. They managed to get the lid off, and inside they found what they had expected: blue water. A sip confirmed that it was daily water, and even that had a mild affect, both alleviating wheezing and providing a slight numbing sensation. It left them wanting more, but both resisted. They closed the lid, turning their attention to the containers on the table.

They quickly discussed what they knew so far. The Ascending Day water that Father Bayle administered in his ceremony on the platform above them was potent, the residents of Nabal craving it for both its masking and pleasing qualities. The blue water that they had just tasted was neither what they were looking for nor the Ascending Day water, and they still didn't know why Ascending Day water was different. Verdie's clue spurred them on: clear water. By the time the Ascending

Day water reached the mountaintop it was obviously not clear, but how and where it might change was a mystery. The containers on the table fueled their curiosity, and taking the pry bar with him, Brenton followed Joe up the platform steps.

"There are only two sizes of casks," said Joe, quickly sizing up the situation. "Look here!" he exclaimed, reaching the table, pointing to one of the larger casks.

The letters "FB" could be seen on all the larger casks, while the smaller casks were marked "Nutrition Bureau." One was already partially open. Next to it lay a small measuring cup with a flat handle; the cup was stained blue. Brenton stepped up, slid the lid aside and looked into the container, Joe right beside him. As Brenton tilted the container, a thick, blue liquid oozed forward.

"Be careful!" warned Joe.

His suspicion about an additive expressed earlier that day was fresh in his mind. They exchanged a quick glance, and then Joe cautiously dipped the tip of his little finger in the solution, the blue ooze sticking readily. He hesitated before he touched finger to tip of tongue, then his face crinkled and he pursed his lips, spitting on the ground and wiping what remained onto the table.

"That has to be poison," he asserted, the liquid immediately numbing the tip of his tongue. A pleasant rush touched his body, and his thinking temporarily clouded, but the worst of it passed quickly, and he found that he still had his wits about him. "That's a strong solution," he added. "It must be mixed with clear water right here."

His deduction about the containers labeled "FB" was clear to him, and he just had to open one container to confirm his suspicions. Before they moved on, Joe took out a flask and carefully filled it with the blue substance, wanting to have the evidence of its existence. Although he had no idea how that evidence might be used, the chances of finding it again were slim.

Their wheezing worsened as they worked, adding urgency to the task at hand, and Brenton moved on. The first three larger containers were empty; the fourth sloshed as he shook it. The fifth and sixth were full, but just as Brenton and Joe were prepared to open one, they heard the kitchen door slam and a distinct, familiar sound reached their ears; they could clearly make out the click of Father Bayle's boots.

Joe and Brenton froze. Father Bayle's dog was soon at the door, yapping, and in the background, in low tones, Father Bayle coaxed the dog to calm down. They heard the sound of cupboards closing, and then the kitchen door closing again, then again, and now there were several voices.

What if Father Bayle comes into the storehouse? Brenton thought to himself.

Their options were extremely limited; hiding among the casks with the dog nearby would be out of the question. Concealment was not their biggest problem, however, because with the kitchen occupied they had no way out of the cavernous space, and their symptoms were steadily worsening.

"Let's take the casks with us!" Joe exclaimed in a forceful whisper.

"We have to!" responded Brenton.

Soon both climbing packs bulged with a container, and as they searched for escape Brenton spotted some stairs beyond the platform, leading to a door. He went as quickly and quietly as he could to the end of the platform, ran off the stage and up the steps, but the door was locked. While Brenton ran to test the door, Joe was summing up their dilemma, and by the time Brenton returned Joe had the answer.

"Up!" he urged, jabbing with an upraised finger.

"Of course!" whispered Brenton, looking up at the winding stair, straining to see the hatch in the dim light. "It has to open from inside!"

The storehouse prisoners secured their packs and moved quickly toward the winding stair. Brenton grabbed a small pry bar from the table, tucking it into a coat pocket. They were soon atop the auditorium, moving fast, passing a box connected to the dangling rope on their way to the spiral stair. They began climbing, pausing momentarily now and again to rest tired legs and breathe; by now both were reaching a severe stage of wheezing. They didn't hear the lock turn in the door, or the door open, but they did hear Yap's namesake sound suddenly get louder, and they both stopped and looked down; a pale trapezoid of yellow light spilled onto the floor of the huge storeroom.

In came Yap, bright red leash fully taxed, followed by his crimson-clad benefactor, who was leaning back to offset canine enthusiasm. One arm appeared a wider extension of the leash, while the other clutched to robed breast a loaf and a tall, blue bottle. The master began a deliberate crossing of the warehouse floor toward the back door to his office; Yap had other ideas. The little dog tried to climb the stairs to the platform where Brenton and Joe had made their first discovery, and he pulled the crimson arm wide, hopping awkwardly sideways as the duo crossed below nervous eyes. Father Bayle had no reason to suspect that Yap was indeed on to something, and it never occurred to him to look up. Had he done so, he might have caught the dim blur of two figures, frozen amongst the iron-works, high above the box-like auditorium. Brenton and Joe were perfectly still, straining mentally and physically to manage the sickness that was slowly killing them, their need for healing becoming desperation. Father Bayle finished his crossing, cajoling and coercing the little ball of excited fur up the stair, and then a key turned, a door opened and shut, and the click of the lock signaled an end to the danger.

Rested, but wheezing severely and feeling helplessly mortal, the climbers continued their quest for escape, and reaching the top of the stair with much effort, they slumped briefly on the landing to rest beside a short ladder leading up to the dearest symbol of freedom either had ever seen.

Their relief was short lived, however, when they heard muffled voices outside the hatch, and just above them on the dais, scraping boots. A heavy object rumbling across the surface made Joe think it was a clean up crew; it appeared that their quest for freedom would soon be over. Going back down was out of the question, and both patients were becoming faint from straining against the wheezing; with chests tightening, they were now struggling to get enough air to think clearly. Brenton reasoned that there was only one thing to do, and he whispered,

"Let's open one of the containers. I won't last much longer."

Whoever was outside could come through the hatch at any moment. The two could not climb back down, but if they hoped to survive, come what may, at that moment drinking water of any composition was their only hope. A pack was coming off when above them boots left the platform, and a moment later the rumble of a cart could be heard going across the mountaintop toward the ramp. Soon they could hear the cart on the ramp, passing them on the outside and going down toward the Village floor. They decided to move.

Joe led the pair up the ladder, fumbling with the latch in the near-darkness, trying desperately to understand the mechanism by touch, and soon he had it. He pushed upward until it locked in place. Pale sunlight streamed into the cavern, illuminating Joe and Brenton on the ladder, blinding them.

When eyes adjusted, each thought the other had aged considerably, and although neither had ever been this sick, both knew that aging was an extreme symptom, signaling imminent death. Joe peeked out cautiously. He could hear the rumble of the cart rolling down the ramp clinging to the side of the mountain, so he quickly scrambled out and turned to help Brenton. Joe pulled him out of the hatch, removed Brenton's pack, helping him sit on the dais. They were free from their prison in the belly of the mountain, and Joe took off his own pack, pulling out the cask. Fumbling in his coat pocket for the pry bar, Brenton handed it to Joe, and the two looked anxiously at each other before Joe turned to the cask.

In spite of his weakness Joe worked quickly and soon the lid on the little wooden cask labeled "FB" popped up. Exchanging a furtive glance, they both peered in, and there they saw something neither had seen before: clear water.

5. Above the Apartments of Father Bayle

Brenton and Joe were back on the mountaintop. Earlier the climb had been imposed on them, and they had rejected the polluted water offered by Father Bayle. Now they had come by choice, ready to accept what they hoped was unpolluted water. They believed that they had found the water referred to in the little note from Verdie, not knowing what the affects of drinking "only clear water" would be. They both reached for the container and Joe got to it first. He smiled as he often did, and handed it to Brenton.

"I want you to have it first. You need it more than I do."

Brenton's cheeks flushed. "I..." Brenton started, but Joe held up a hand

"It's OK," he said.

Brenton's intent had been to grab the container and take the first drink; Joe meant to get to it first so he could give the first drink.

Accepting the gift, and now desperate for healing, Brenton lifted the cask to his lips. He took in two mouthfuls, gulping desperately for life, then paused, immediately feeling the water's touch. He felt it, not just controlling his symptoms, but reaching into a still, deep place, like a balm to his being, the very essence of who he was; the realization was far deeper and more profound than anything he had ever experienced.

Whereas the drugged water of the Village affected his mind by imposing euphoria, he knew quite suddenly that the clear water set his mind free to sense the pleasure of healing power and wholeness on its own. Something deep and essential was at work here, and he wanted more of it, not just to erase symptoms, but because his mind was suddenly released, from what he did not know, and it was clearer than it had ever been. He sat in silence as something he hadn't felt since childhood came over him; he remembered joy.

Next to him, Joe had taken two gulps and was having a similar experience. As the two sat in silence looking at each other, their appearances changed, both looking healthy again. They smiled and felt like laughing for the first time in a long time, but they held back. They were exposed on the mountaintop, and still had to figure out how to remain undetected until they could get down the mountain, and home. They sat there for a time before one of them spoke.

"I wonder if we're healed?" Brenton ventured, feeling that in that moment, on that mountaintop, the disease must surely have been conquered.

"I don't know," Joe mused. "Verdie's note just told us to drink clear water today. There was no promise of healing."

His mind perfectly clear now, Brenton remembered each element of the note.

"That's true," he said. "She also hinted at something more real than what we sense. To find it we had to climb with her. It feels like I've climbed and found really real."

Joe thought before speaking. "You didn't climb with her, though. What if there's something even better?"

Brenton mulled the idea. "I think I could just live with this. It seems good enough."

He paused for a moment as his new reality began to take hold, the mundane every-day momentarily distant and surreal, but ever present.

"I don't know what we're going to do about daily water; I don't ever want that filthy blue stuff in me again."

Joe agreed and then went on.

"If there is better than what we usually sense, I want that!" he said, and then added thoughtfully, "I want that for you, Brenton, no matter what it would take."

Brenton had no idea how Joe's mind worked, and he hadn't felt joy or happiness for a long time, but he was happy he had a friend like Joe.

Joe was thinking beyond the moment now.

"Let's save as much of this as possible," he counseled, sealing the container. "We have to learn how clear water works."

They had no idea how long the healing effects would last, how much to drink, or how often. Joe was eager to move on now that he was feeling strong and as good as he ever had, and he secured the container and stowed it.

They rose and moved cautiously to the edge of the space and looked around. There was little movement on the streets below, as most residents had returned to their homes as was their custom at the end of the workday, or following public gatherings. The Plant lay silent and lifeless below them, and Brenton wondered aloud about taking the clear water to work undetected.

They could see into the gated courtyard of the Nutrition Bureau where an unusual number of grey-uniformed men were moving.

"Have you ever been inside there?" Brenton was pointing.

Joe shook his head. "I don't know anyone who has."

As they watched, the men formed lines and began a drill. It was hard to tell what was going on, but it was obviously organized.

A lone rider moved past the men and out of the courtyard, making his way directly to the Village gate. Then he was off at a brisk trot down the dusty road toward the ranch.

They agreed that they should wait for the cover of dark before descending, as climbing Mt. Nabal unaccompanied was not allowed. All the more, they did not want to arouse any suspicions considering their cargo.

They made their way around the wall, now at a more leisurely pace and less awkward stance than a few hours before. As they came around to face The Mountain, Brenton was brought up short; the Mountain was brighter, or starker, and somehow more real than it had looked earlier in the day. As if jarred by the sight of The Mountain, the fleeting memory that had eluded him the night before came back more completely. He remembered the pictures—now more vivid—in the storybooks that his mother had read to him about the old days. But now he remembered more, and The Mountain was prominent in them. There was something else about the pictures that he knew was important, but he couldn't quite recall it. He had always been attracted to adventure as a boy, but over time many of his memories had faded completely. He was remembering Verdie too, and how she liked the same books, and he wondered if she was living an adventure. Drinking clear water seemed to be healing his mind as well as his body, as dormant memories began to volunteer themselves.

"The Mountain seems more real," Joe said simply.

Standing next to Brenton, Joe had been staring at The Mountain too and voiced what they were both observing.

Joe was staring at The Mountain as he spoke again.

"I'm not sure what it means for certain, but everything today seems to be pointing to The Mountain."

Brenton thought of Father Bayle and his warnings about The Mountain and its people. Because of him, Brenton had always avoided contact with Helpers and even the innocuous Climbers, even though most kept homes in Nabal. He had always believed Father Bayle about The Mountain and its dangers, but after the day's events he was beginning to question many things in his world. In spite of Brenton's growing doubts and suspicions, Joe seemed to be going further, hinting at something Brenton wasn't ready for.

His thoughts turned to his house, and with it that practiced longing to be home and safe behind the gates and locks. *Going to my secure job at the Plant every day is tolerable,* he thought, beginning to argue with himself and justify his choices. He remembered the upcoming Preservation Reward that was due him from the Banking Bureau, and he thought—all of a sudden his healing mind threw a completely different thought at him; his comfort and safety in Nabal was dependent on tainted water. He had tasted something better, but he couldn't get more. That idea turned his thoughts back to The Mountain, to Verdie and her note, and to his adventurous friend next to him at the wall.

"Do you know anyone who has been there?" Brenton asked as they stared across the arid Flatlands to the strangely prominent Mountain and its encircling lake.

"Only Verdie," Joe responded quietly. "I talked to a Helper once. He seemed kind enough, and I didn't sense any danger from him."

The two couldn't think about The Mountain, or anything associated with it, without the specter of Father Bayle and his warnings imposing itself. Joe went on.

"I know some Climbers. They're safe and they don't seem that different from anyone else – except that they live most of the time at The Mountain."

Brenton was listening, but his attention was drawn to some movement on the road a short distance from the Village; it appeared to be a small group of people walking together, their bright clothes a sharp contrast to the drab landscape. Brenton pointed them out to Joe, who smiled.

"Maybe they're Helpers," Joe said hopefully.

Brenton looked at The Mountain again and brought up clear water.

"Do you think the clear water comes from that lake?" he asked.

Joe had been quietly organizing his thoughts, and he turned to his friend.

"I don't know where it comes from, but I know we need to find out. Here's what I do know." Joe was concentrating, staring at some point on the wall as he spoke, his hands moving with his words as he began to carefully lay out what he had been mulling. "Verdie left. Father Bayle protested. She sent us a note marked with a pickaxe symbol, an invitation to climb to find what is really Real, and a hint about clear water. I experimented with not drinking blue water, my mind cleared. We climbed this morning and didn't drink, and both our minds cleared. We got lucky and found blue poison and "clear water." We drank it and got instant healing, clear minds, and something deep inside changed. The Mountain looks different. Neither of us wants blue water. We have no source for clear water, but we have pretty clear evidence where that source is." He paused, looked up briefly at Brenton, then turned back to The Mountain.

Brenton listened, and he couldn't disagree, Joe's words making their course seem clear. He thought over the facts as they stood there silently, but as stark and obvious as Joe's reasoning seemed to be, a moment later it wasn't obvious at all. Doubt rose like a veil, while uncertainty clouded his thinking, and paralyzing fear held his mind in an icy grip. *What about my life in Nabal? My house? My job? What if we can't find the source? What will Father Bayle do to us? How could we find enough water to cross the Flatlands?* That longing for his house, his locks, his safety, and the Preservation Reward came over him again. He even thought about his little bird, singing in the cage he had made.

Having a clear mind and seeing things as they really are means tough choices, Brenton thought. He realized that he had hardly any choices to make in Nabal, and that thought led him to think of the blue water, and he wondered if the water was even worse than they believed. *What did Father Bayle know?*

The thought rose in his mind that he had never seen Father Bayle wheeze, and he remembered the "FB" printed on the cask he was carrying. He thought of that beautiful, clear water, and he wanted more, and not just a drink; he wanted enough beautiful water to last a lifetime. It dawned on his healing mind that, like joy, he hadn't thought of anything as beautiful for a long time.

"We have to go to The Mountain." Joe's matter-of-fact conclusion had an air of finality.

That statement brought the battle in Brenton's mind to a temporary truce. After all of the evidence and the long silence, Brenton knew this was coming. In the space of less than a day his ideas about truth were being shattered, and now new thoughts were emerging, gently prodding him to the next step: action.

"You're right, Joe..." Brenton's soft response trailed off. "And I don't want to be afraid anymore."

Joe was smiling as he turned to put a hand on Brenton's shoulder.

"Me either," he said simply.

The setting sun, under-lighting a bank of low clouds, shed eerie orange light on the companions standing on the simulated mountaintop, directly above the apartments of Father Bayle. Across the expanse of the Flatlands, The Mountain, bold and clear in the fading light, looked beautiful and inviting, its encircling lake glittering like a jeweled ring.

As the two stood far above him, seated at his expansive table in his crimson robe with a tall, blue bottle and leashed companion comfortably within reach, in healing minds the specter of Father Bayle was gone.

6. Father Bayle's Boys

Night was falling, the moon rising as resolve and hope grew in the minds and hearts of the pair making their way quietly down the ramp. The memory of the sound of boots on the ramp now tempered their haste to descend.

"How are your symptoms?" Joe wondered.

Brenton was feeling fine and said so. They were just beginning to learn about clear water, and the contrast between how they had felt before and after taking a drink had been the topic of conversation. Now talk turned to pressing matters.

Brenton had a question. "Do you have an idea of what to do next?"

"We should go soon, but I'm worried about having enough water to cross the Flatlands."

Brenton had the same concern; they had to keep their symptoms at bay. He had a thought.

"At first I was afraid we couldn't carry enough, but maybe this clear water will make it possible to cross, even though we have so little."

Joe thought the idea plausible, and had already begun to shape a plan; he hesitated, and then spoke his mind.

"I think we should leave tonight," he said, unsure of Brenton's reaction.

Brenton was glad to hear Joe's thoughts, as delaying would increase risk, primarily because of water; they had to be decisive, and that was new to him. They needed to find the source, but they had to think through the barriers to their goal quickly.

"It's so much to take in," Brenton said, and he thought of Father Bayle. "Should we talk to him first?" Brenton was allowing his fear to speak.

Joe stopped, resting a hand on Brenton's arm.

"What do you think he would say?"

Brenton thought of Verdie, and the answer was obvious. Brenton had overcome imposed fear of The Mountain, and at some point he would have to overcome his fear of Father Bayle. For now, the last thing they needed was Father Bayle's involvement in their plans; even his knowledge of their plans might bring them to ruin.

Joe was thinking of their friends.

"What shall we tell Mark and Meyer?" he asked near the landing.

Brenton thought for a moment. "We have been invited to visit a friend, and we are going to be gone a few days, but nothing else," he suggested.

"I think you're right," Joe agreed. "Let's do that first."

Brenton had an idea that there would be a brief visit to The Mountain, and that if they did find clear water, they might find a way to bring a supply home, or form a plan for a regular resupply. He expressed his thoughts to Joe.

"I don't know what we will find, Brenton. We do know that Verdie cares about us, and she has given us new information, so we should believe that she is trying to help us, and hope."

Cautiously looking around, they reached the bottom of the ramp. Back on the Village floor, no longer intrepid adventurers, they became two Villagers out for a stroll. They went quickly to Joe's to stow their climbing packs, not wanting to arouse any suspicion, and then set off in the direction of Mark's house.

They were too busy thinking ahead to look behind, or they might have seen two grey figures keeping a safe distance.

Joe and Brenton were discussing the logistics of the journey as they reached the little house near the Plant with a gated arbor. Mark responded to the knock at the gate. As they entered the house they found Meyer, who had been chatting with Mark over a beer. Mark offered one to Brenton and Joe who politely declined, not wanting to take any chances with Village food or drink. Joe apologized for not waiting for Mark and Meyer after the climb, telling them that he and Brenton had chores and errands. He added that Brenton had won the bet.

Neither seemed offended, replying that they had business of their own after the climb.

Feeling anxious for the journey ahead, Brenton spoke.

"We came for a reason, and we were going to visit you, too, Meyer." He had their attention, and went on. "We have received an invitation to visit a friend, so we are going to be gone for several days. We're not sure how long."

As he said this, Brenton realized the foolishness of his intended ruse, as Mark and Meyer would know any friend of his. He had been unsure if they might alert Father Bayle if they knew the truth. Mark looked at Meyer, who responded first.

"A friend?" Meyer asked. "Is her name Verdie?"

He stared at them blankly as Brenton and Joe exchanged a quick glance. Brenton was stunned. *How had Meyer figured out their plan? Who else might know?* Mark and Meyer were much closer to Father Bayle than he and Joe, and they consulted him on everything.

Brenton started to ask, "How did...?"

"How did I know about Verdie?" Meyer interrupted.

He and Mark looked at each other again and simultaneously pulled a little wrapped invitation from their pockets. Brenton was relieved; Joe blew out a breath.

Meyer went on.

"I said we had business of our own today. We spent a good deal of time this afternoon with Father Bayle."

That he had talked to Father Bayle was no surprise. as Mark and Meyer spent time with Father Bayle regularly, and he took a special interest in them. Mark and Meyer were the needy sons of a cloying father.

Father Bayle had at one time taken the four friends—five, including Verdie—into his expansive apartments at the Mountain Club. According to the Health Bureau, an unfortunate outbreak in the Village affected older Villagers most severely, and the young people had lost their parents. Father Bayle had taken the group of orphans into his apartments, helping them through their teens and young adulthood and eventually helping them get jobs at the Plant and houses in the Village.

The five had become fast friends with common bonds of loss and proximity. Mark and Meyer were very close to Father Bayle, while the others, though remaining polite, over time distanced themselves. Verdie had escaped his umbrella, while Joe actively looked for and pointed out contradictions, and Brenton, once neutral, was now wary of possible duplicity at best, his healing mind suspecting even worse.

"Have you talked to Father Bayle about your trip?" asked Mark.

Before answering, Joe had an idea, and a question.

"Do you mind if I see your notes?" he asked calmly.

The two unwrapped their notes, and Joe looked them over and breathed a sigh of relief. The notes were one-sided, and simply said,

Come visit me!

Verdie

Joe answered Mark's question. "No, we haven't talked to Father Bayle yet," he said.

Brenton had a question, driven by his growing suspicions.

"What did Father Bayle think of your invitations?" he asked.

Meyer responded. "We didn't know where Verdie went, but Father Bayle told us that she went to The Mountain."

"We decided not to go. It's too dangerous," added Mark. "Are you sure you're going to go? Father Bayle doesn't think anyone should go near it."

Joe was thinking quickly. "Oh, she's at The Mountain?"

Assuming that the two would talk to Father Bayle about the visit, Joe wanted him to think that it was Mark and Meyer who told them where Verdie was, not wanting Father Bayle to suspect that there was more information on their invitations.

"We were going to ask Father Bayle," Joe added, sealing the deception.

Brenton answered Mark's concerns. "If Verdie is OK, I don't see how it can be too dangerous to visit. We'll only stay a few days."

He said nothing further about Father Bayle or his objections. He wondered why Father Bayle was so adamant about keeping Villagers, and especially Verdie, from The Mountain. The protestations about The Mountain drove Brenton's curiosity and his desire for adventure, and he was eager to leave.

"We should be going," Brenton said, looking at Joe.

"When are you leaving on your trip?" asked Meyer.

Joe was ready. "Tonight, as soon as we can."

Brenton snapped a look at him.

"Travel safely," said Mark, without reiterating his concerns.

"Please give Verdie our love," added Meyer. She had been like a little sister to them, and they all missed her.

Joe and Brenton moved toward the door, and Mark let them out with some final goodbyes. They moved under the arbor and into the street with the high, bright moon lighting their way.

Brenton spoke first. "We didn't even think about them getting invitations. I wonder why the notes were different?"

"That will be a good question to ask Verdie when we see her. She was closer to you and I, and she knows how close those two are to Father Bayle. There appears to be much more going on around us than we've discovered so far."

Joe was smiling and thinking ahead. The game was afoot, and he was beginning to enjoy it.

"Why did you tell them we're leaving tonight?" Brenton asked.

"There was no harm in it. I know them—those two will wait to tell him in the morning, and by then we'll be gone."

Brenton wasn't sure about Joe's rationale, but he didn't object. The hint of some kind of conspiracy against them, along with the events of the day, made Brenton think of the storybooks from his childhood, filled with stories of adventure. He wondered briefly where the books were, and if he would ever see them again. Then he thought of Verdie, and his pace quickened.

Behind them, a tall figure stepped out of deep shadow and let himself through the bramble-covered gate at the little house near the Plant, a flash of crimson in the bright moonlight.

On The Motivating Force of Hope

Uncertainty and doubt prevail
Where hope has found no foothold
No light shines out from future's door
No call to pathways yet untold
But hope, once seen, if but a glimpse
Transcends the stagnant present
To bid us move, to push, keep on
'Til joy is hope's fulfillment

7. Unexpected Company

Arriving at Joe's house, the two carefully poured water from one cask into four flasks, then Joe hid the container under some floorboards. Brenton helped Joe pack up food, clothes and bedding. They locked up and made their way to Brenton's house. Even on Ascending Day letters were delivered, and Brenton had received a notice from the Banking Bureau; his Preservation Reward audit was imminent. He hurriedly shoved it in a pocket as they went inside, Brenton kicking worn boots off tired feet and removing his warm jacket.

They filled four flasks with the second cask and there was a little left over so they decided to drink it just before leaving. Their symptoms still had not returned, and they had great hope that they had been healed or very close to it. Brenton hid the cask, and then rummaged in the pantry. Between them they had food for three days—they hoped it would be enough. Brenton quickly packed his things, including his stash of coins, and wondered if he was taking too much baggage.

The little bird, disturbed by the packing commotion, flapped wings and ruffled feathers. Brenton looked at it, his clearing mind wondering that he had never noticed how beautiful it was. He felt sorry that he had kept it captive, so he stepped out the back door and opened the cage. The bird hesitated, then seized the opportunity and escaped into the night.

They finished preparations and Brenton sat down to pull his woeful boots back on. They were not well made, and he would need new shoes soon, but the Plant would not issue them until the old ones had broken down completely. After the boots, Brenton pulled on his favorite jacket.

Brenton's forest-green jacket was the only thing that he had from his father's belongings. It was unusual in the Flatlands and was too well made to have come from the Plant. One day, soon after he had moved in to his house, a small package arrived. Opening it he found a note that simply said:

"This jacket belonged to your father."

He never knew where it came from or where other family belongings had gone. Father Bayle had a strange reaction whenever he saw Brenton wearing it.

Joe and Brenton helped each other shoulder packs; they were both bringing a considerable load, inexperienced as they were at travel. They drained cups of clear water, immediately feeling invigorated and ready for adventure.

Outside, Brenton locked up the house and gates, wondering when he would see his little cottage again. The moon was bright in the clear sky as they turned down the street to the next corner and then turned south to skirt Mt. Nabal and the open center of town. Alternating west and south streets, sometimes taking quiet paths under leafless trees, they made their way silently toward the Village gate. They passed no one, late as it was.

Near the town gate they paused at the edge of the open plaza. They looked around but saw no one. Brenton shuddered at the silence of the eerie, dark streets as they moved to the gate which was large and heavy but never locked, as Father Bayle had proudly mentioned the night before. They were indeed free to come and go, and they exercised their freedom by pushing the gate open, the old portal creaking loudly in protest. But they slipped through, and they were free of the Village.

They paused, looking around, breathing in their newfound freedom. They were out of the Village with healthy minds for the first time in memory. They looked down the road, into the unknown, and then looked at each other in the bright moonlight.

"Are you ready?" asked Joe.

Brenton felt more than ready as the reality of their quest was settling in.

He smiled and confidently said, "Yes, let's go."

Brenton took an exaggerated slow first step, and they were off down the dusty road.

They didn't notice the grey, hooded figure move silently away from the Village wall, slipping into the Flatlands north of the road.

The Village was situated on a low rise, and the moonlit Flatlands were laid out before them. Low hills, scrub, and small scattered trees could be seen, dull and grey in the moonlight as they made their way down the hill, the occasional rock formation jutting out of grey earth like broken teeth. As they reached the bottom of the hill, the sunken road was bordered on each side by a low berm, preventing continuous views into the Flatlands. Leaving the Village behind, they talked quietly about what might lie ahead.

They hadn't gone far when they both thought they heard the creaky Village gate, so they stopped, Brenton resisting an urge to crouch. They turned, straining to see who else might be out at this time of night. Brenton could make out two figures in the moonlight, moving their way. They were burdened and lumbering, and soon one of the two called out.

"Wait!" came the familiar voice. It was Meyer.

Soon the four heavily laden friends were facing each other, two of them out of breath. Brenton gave them a moment before asking the obvious.

"Where are you going?"

"We want to go with you to The Mountain. We want to see Verdie," Mark answered.

Brenton and Joe looked at each other.

"We changed our minds and thought you could use the company," added Meyer.

Brenton was skeptical. "What about Father Bayle's warnings?" He had never known them to defy Father Bayle's advice.

Meyer answered this time. "We talked it over and agreed that if Verdie is OK and wants us to visit, it must not be dangerous."

Meyer's rationale wasn't his own, but since Brenton had spoken the words himself, there could be no objection.

Brenton considered his thoughts on Mt. Nabal warring for dominance earlier in the day. *Ideas don't change that easily,* he thought.

Joe asked the practical question. "Did you bring enough water?"

There was no possibility that Joe and Brenton could share the clear water and reveal what they knew. At least not yet.

"Yes, we have plenty of water," Mark assured him.

Joe wondered how they could have had as much as they needed, as they could not have resupplied so late in the evening.

Brenton and Joe gave no voice to their skepticism, so they accepted the unexpected company, and Joe filled them in.

"We're going to walk a while, then leave the road, make a fire, and get a spell of sleep."

Brenton noticed that Mark was looking over his shoulder toward the middle of town and Mt. Nabal, and he wondered if Mark was having second thoughts.

The friends moved off, silent as they walked, and Brenton wondered what this development would mean, and at what point their companions might discover clear water. *How would we tell them how we discovered it?* Brenton thought.

The Mountain loomed ahead of them, its dark presence defined by the moonlit clouds shrouding the unknowable peak.

Joe was thinking about food and water as they walked, hoping that Mark and Meyer had enough for themselves, and soon they were wheezing slightly, sipping from flasks. Joe decided to feign a drink, pushing off the inevitable, and Brenton picked up on the idea.

They had walked a good distance, the moon was low in the sky, and Mt. Nabal was barely visible behind them when the companions passed through a section of road where they could see over the berm to the north. The land was mostly flat, with a few low round hills, some with rock formations jutting into the night sky. To the north and west, slightly ahead of them, Brenton thought he saw a flicker of orange light illuminating rocks on the crown of a hill. He mentioned his suspicion to the group, and Brenton and Joe climbed the berm, waiting for the others. Mark and Meyer whispered something, then joined them. They were all looking in the direction that Brenton indicated when they saw the orange light. They had come across no other travelers, or any other signs of life since they left Nabal, and because of the lack of water there were no farms or homesteads in the open lands. Knowing this, Brenton wondered aloud what they had seen, and asked Joe what he thought they should do.

"Find out what's up there," he replied, smiling.

Mark and Meyer were less intrepid and glanced at each other but followed nonetheless.

They set off in the direction of the light, winding down from the berm through a small valley. They began climbing the suspect rise hindered by clumped grasses and scree, but before long they approached the top. Flickering orange light painted rocks across a small hollow, a fire ablaze in it, unseen but distinctly heard as they approached.

They were completely unprepared for any possible hostility. Joe was in the lead and motioned the group to hands and knees.

They crawled and, reaching the rim, sweet, soft laughter rose out of the hollow, mingling with sparks and firelight—a woman's laughter, a sound long forgotten by the weary travelers. Across the hollow on the far grassy bank sat a woman with long, curly blonde hair. She looked confident and kind, she was lithe and strong, and a grey cloak with a hood lay beside her. She was looking right at them, beaming, and though they sensed no danger, they were cautious.

"All is well. You may come to the edge," she said reassuringly, her voice soft and strong. Brenton had a feeling that he had heard and seen her before. Rising, they saw two more women lying by the fire, one under light coverings, stirring at the unfolding conversation, the other lying on her back with hands behind her head, looking up at the rim. Both women sat up. They were all similarly dressed in light colored vests, with light pants cropped just below the knee, and they wore sturdy shoes, beautifully decorated with bright studs circling a triad of pickaxes on the top. Near the fire, a trio of long-handled pickaxes leaned together on the grassy carpet of the hollow.

Joe was the first traveler to speak. "You're Helpers!" he exclaimed.

The woman on the far bank rose.

"We are," she said. "You know your Mountain people, I see." She spoke through a perpetual smile, and Brenton thought of Verdie.

One of the women by the fire spoke. "You are Brenton, Joe, Mark and Meyer, but I have no knowledge of who is who."

The companions looked at each other, eyebrows raised and mouths open, and the women chuckled at the expressions on startled faces.

The speaker had dark hair in tight rings, and very dark skin. Brenton had never seen skin as dark, and he thought it beautiful.

"We are Cara, Natia, and Leila, but you must guess who is who." More laughter rang in the hollow as the third woman spoke. She was now sitting with her arms around her knees, and she appeared lean and tall, her long, raven hair falling around strong shoulders.

"Will you come down by the fire? I am Cara," the blond woman said. "You are loud; I saw you before you were in the valley."

It was a tease, not a boast, and she laughed again as they descended into the hollow, lowering packs onto the green grass.

The women rearranged their things, and soon everyone found a place around the fire.

"Welcome to camp," said the woman with the long black hair, smiling. "I am Natia." She appeared to be the youngest.

"Hello, Leila," Joe said, greeting the dark skinned woman. The women all smiled at his joke.

"How do you know us?" Joe asked for the group, all of them curious.

"First, put names to faces." Cara appeared to be leading, and each told her their name in turn, and then she continued. "Do you know a young woman named Verdie?"

Joe and Brenton looked at each other.

"The invitations! You brought us the invitations!" It was Brenton who figured it out.

Mark and Meyer weren't saying anything, as they had been drinking drugged water, and minds were sluggish. They had been warned over and over about the danger of Helpers, but here they were experiencing the most melodic laughter and kind faces they had ever encountered; they were conflicted and confused.

Brenton sensed a bond, an attraction to these free spirits, and he had never felt anything like it. Their confidence, the quick laughter, and the joy they showed built immediate trust. Brenton wanted to ask about invitations and clear water, but not in front of Mark and Meyer. He chose common ground.

"How is Verdie?" He wanted to hear for certain that she was well.

"Verdie is quite well," smiled Cara. "She wants to see you all, and we were happy to be of help. That is what we do!" All three Helpers laughed.

Mark finally spoke.

"I've been told all my life that Helpers are dangerous." The slow, blunt comment was out of place, but the women weren't fazed.

"Whoever told you that was correct," smiled Leila. "We are very dangerous." She meant it, but no one felt it. "We are of no danger to you, however. We only want to be of help to you."

Brenton noticed a bow and arrow stowed with packs at the edge of firelight, recognized from pictures in storybooks. He turned back to Cara.

"You came to the Village just to bring us invitations to see Verdie?"

Cara, staring at the fire, turned to look at him. "Yes," she said, still smiling.

"What are you doing out here now?" Brenton was trying to understand the situation.

"Today, we were watching for you." She did not say what they might be doing on other days, and Brenton sensed finality in her answer.

Joe remembered seeing figures on the road from Mt. Nabal. "Were you near the Village today, on the road?"

Natia brushed her long hair back as she looked at Joe. "You have strong eyes," she said softly.

Brenton thought Joe blushed.

Meyer looked at Joe, his sluggish mind straining. "How did you know that, Joe?" he finally asked.

Joe didn't want to reveal too much, but he could answer truthfully. "When we were on the mountain, I thought I saw movement on the road."

That satisfied Meyer.

Cara preempted any more conversation, her voice kind.

"Surely, you must be tired. Unpack what you need for your comfort. We will speak more in the morning."

The tired travelers made no complaint as Cara motioned the Helpers out of earshot. Moments later, while the weary group found comfort by the fire and pulled coats about them, Leila selected a bow and quiver. She climbed out of the hollow and moved in the direction of the road; Cara and Natia lay down to rest.

Watching Leila disappear into the night, Brenton turned to Joe and whispered, "Why would she need a bow, and why do we need a guard?"

"I said it once earlier tonight," Joe responded, "there appears to be much more going on around us than we've discovered so far."

On the brow of the hill, Leila pulled her grey hood over her curly hair as she nestled in among some rocks. She faced the road, her bow at the ready; Cara had done her part that night, and now it was her turn.

8. Such Sweet Sorrow

The sun was barely touching the low hill, soft yellow light illuminating mist above the hollow and casting a golden glow over the campers who lay sleeping, as the low fire gently warmed dreams.

His companions were still asleep when Brenton woke. He wheezed mildly; a mouthful from a flask was welcome relief. He closed his eyes and focused on healing water, feeling peaceful and full of hope for the journey ahead.

In his relaxed mind a blonde woman suddenly appeared, hands covering face, sobbing.

He paused, reviewing the vision before rising.

Cara and Natia were speaking softly on the far side of the grassy hollow, and as Brenton stood up, Cara beckoned, her face lit with a characteristic smile. As he approached, she said,

"Good day," speaking just above a whisper.

"Good day, Cara," he responded, "and to you, Natia," he added.

"I must speak on a matter of importance," she told him. "I see that you and Joe are not wheezing like the others, and you think more clearly. So you found it?"

Brenton was still foggy, but it took only a moment to understand.

"Yes!" came his enthusiastic whisper. "Where does it come from?"

She ignored his question.

"Do the other two know of it?" she asked, brow furrowed.

"No, they don't know anything," Brenton responded.

Her face relaxed. "Do not ask any questions regarding water, or sources, or any such thing," she warned him.

"May I ask why?" Brenton asked, trying to be polite. He had intended to keep the secret as long as possible for his own reasons, but he was curious why it was important to Cara.

"I can only say that the reason is connected to the invitations," she responded. "We did not expect Mark and Meyer, but we were prepared."

Now Brenton was very curious, and he didn't relate the whole story about their visit to Mark's house, but he mentioned that Mark and Meyer had joined in the journey late at night, which caught Cara's interest.

"Father Bayle is their advisor, is he not?"

The feeling that he knew her came back.

"Yes, he is," replied Brenton.

"They are your friends, but you must be careful," Cara said with sincerity.

Brenton nodded as Cara and Natia looked over his shoulder, and Brenton turned to see Mark and Meyer rising. He wanted to get more information from her, but it was not the time to ask. Joe was up, warming hands by the fire, and the Helpers went over to greet the late risers, keeping their voices low for Leila's sake; she had been on guard duty until early light.

"Joe, could you help me with this pack?" Brenton wanted to talk to Joe, so he turned his back to the others and knelt near the packs as Joe came over, and in very low voice related the conversation with Cara.

Joe nodded, and the pair moved back to the fire, where Cara addressed the group.

"I am certain that you want to go soon, but we wish to serve you a meal."

It was a kind offer, and even though they all had food, they accepted. Natia and Cara went to their packs and took out four slender plants, bringing them back to the waiting friends. Brenton had some coins in his hand; the Helpers smiled at the gesture.

"You cannot purchase this food," Cara said. "We have a saying, 'Freely gotten, freely given.'"

Brenton put his coins away.

"This will give you strength," said Natia, peeling a long leaf from the stalk and demonstrating how to eat it.

Mark and Meyer were cautious, but Joe was eager to try something new. He accepted the leaf from Natia, and handed it to Brenton. Smiling at the gesture, Natia handed Joe a whole plant, then she gave one to the others, Brenton last.

As Natia handed him the stalk, Brenton noticed her hand; his name, along with the others, was written there. He paused, staring, and when she realized why, she looked him in the eye. "It is a reminder of our duty."

Brenton accepted the stalk, pulled off a leaf, and ate. He had never tasted anything so good, and he could feel energy rush through his body, affecting him in much the same way as clear water had. Joe was also enjoying his meal, and he and Brenton both thanked their hosts, remarking on the taste. Brenton looked at the other two travelers, who were not eating and trying to be polite about it. Finally Mark spoke.

"This tastes bitter to me."

Brenton saw that Cara and Natia did not react, but simply smiled.

"Perhaps you should give your portion to those who are enjoying it," Cara suggested.

Mark did, and without saying anything, Meyer followed. Mark took a sip of blue water, and choked. Brenton looked at Cara, and she caught his gaze and gave a slight twist of the head with a smile.

Leila woke and greeted everyone warmly. Cara thanked her for doing her duty in the night and had some food ready. Natia massaged an arm that was numb from the way Leila had been sleeping. The Helpers ate as the travelers packed their baggage and prepared for a day on the road. As he packed, Brenton's thoughts turned to Leila and her bow, and that made him think to ask what lay ahead. Cara spoke, smiling because it was her nature.

"The road west holds some dangers," she said. "There are those who would impede travelers who intend to visit The Mountain."

This was news to the group. Mark said,

"Father Bayle said it was dangerous."

Cara had a ready response.

"I believe Father Bayle claims that The Mountain and Helpers are dangerous, not the road to them." It was a soft, motherly correction. "From what you have experienced thus far, you would have no cause to describe me or my companions as dangerous."

Her smile was difficult to resist, and Mark had no defense against its gentle force; he looked at the ground sheepishly, as Cara looked over the group. "Go quickly, stay to the road, keep your goal in mind. That will give you hope."

She paused for a moment, began, caught herself from saying something, and then finished. "You should know that help is never far when you are in need."

"Won't you go with us?" A knot was growing in Brenton's stomach. He had started the journey a naive Villager, and here he was in the wilderness, talking to three strong warriors, unaware of any fight or war or confrontation of any kind since the days of the stories he was beginning to remember.

"No, we cannot accompany you," said Cara. "We have other duties, but I assure you that you will be safe."

"Can we travel through the Flatlands instead of on the road?" Joe wanted alternatives to being exposed.

"I do not advise it," replied Cara. "It is possible to get lost, and though we know the paths and signs, they come with time and practice and shared journeys with those who have gone before."

Her words seemed final, so without further discussion the four thanked their hosts and pulled on their boots, Brenton noting that his were deteriorating badly. They helped each other load packs and climbed out of the hollow amidst warm farewells. Behind them the Helpers immediately broke camp, preparing to move.

The travelers stood briefly on the brow of the hill, surveying the land around them, the sun having cleared the mist that had hung over the hollow at dawn. They could just see Mt. Nabal in the dim east, and turning west, they saw the storage buildings and water towers of the Nutrition Bureau ranch. There was a hill with a plateau around its base across from the ranch, and beyond that The Mountain loomed ever brighter and more real.

All around them the scrub and grasses of the Flatlands dotted the landscape. Low hills and rock outcroppings broke up the flat ground, and they saw no difficult terrain ahead of them or along the road. Whatever dangers they might face, they would not be related to the lay of the land.

The group angled south and west off the hill and soon reached the road. They scrambled down the berm to the sunken grade, pausing for a sip of water before heading west.

Mark used the opportunity to voice concern.

"I think we should turn back. We could be back in Nabal by early afternoon."

Joe looked at him, head cocked to one side.

"Mark, what are you saying? You came running after us last night, begging to come along."

"I think Father Bayle was right—this is too dangerous—for all of us."

Brenton spoke up.

"If you really feel that way, you should go back. I'm afraid too, but I am not turning back."

Mark hesitated.

"All right," he finally said. "I'll go with you, but if I sense danger, I am turning back—and it would be wise for all of you to do the same."

Brenton and Joe looked at each other while Meyer looked away quietly. Without another word, Brenton turned and started down the road, Joe right behind him. First Meyer, then Mark turned west, caught up with the others and kept pace behind them. They walked silently for a time and then stopped for a brief rest at a high point in the road. The berm was low, and for a moment Brenton thought that he saw movement in the scrub off to the north, but he could not be certain. He did see movement in the air—a small black and white bird with an enormously long tail was bobbing along, flying west toward The Mountain.

As they prepared to move on, around a bend in the road ahead of them a solitary traveler emerged; he was loaded down with a pack and bags, and he was dressed as a Climber. The man was walking slowly, head down. He was nearly upon them when he looked up, startled.

"Oh! How far to the Village?" he asked, without greeting.

"A days walk, maybe less," responded Joe. "Where are you coming from?"

"I come from The Mountain," he said. "I lived with the Climbers for a time, but I'm returning to Nabal."

Brenton was thinking about danger. "Have you had any trouble on the road?"

The man thought for a moment. "No, I have had no trouble going east," he said. "The only trouble I have had was at The Mountain. The Climbers' water is better, but little else is different. I am weary, and I want only the safety of my own home."

Brenton remembered his own thoughts the day before. He wanted to ask about water, but before he could, Mark asked,

"Do you advise us to turn back?"

"That is for you to decide. I cannot tell you your path. Each man's journey is his own. Mine takes me back to the Village. Farewell."

He began lumbering past them, east toward the Village.

Brenton spoke to the others. "This man couldn't stay at The Mountain for his own reasons. We've learned nothing more. We should go."

Mark resisted. "We should go with him. He shouldn't be alone, and we should go no farther. I'm worried about my water. We've been told all our lives to stay near the source."

Joe had heard enough.

"Mark, as your friend, I advise you—no, I tell you—turn back now and go with him. Go back to the Village, to your home and safety, and leave us to go on the journey that we have chosen. I can't abide any more whining. You are not ready to take this journey."

Mark looked west toward The Mountain, then east after the woeful traveler.

"I can't go on," he admitted, then he looked at the three friends. "You should all come with me."

Brenton recalled his conversation with Cara, and it appeared to him that Mark had never intended to go to The Mountain. It was as if some other will had imposed itself on him.

"I'm sorry to see you go, Mark, but I am not turning back," Brenton said staunchly.

Mark looked from Brenton to Joe, and then at Meyer, who had nothing to say except farewell. Mark wished them all safety on their journey and asked them to greet Verdie for him. He turned back toward the Village, calling after the traveler ahead of him; the man stopped and looked back. He waited for Mark who caught up with him, and then turning toward the three in the road, Mark waved.

The two deflated travelers turned and began their long walk back to the comfort and safety of the Village, the pleasant poison issued by the Water Dispensary, and the guiding hand of Father Bayle.

On The Battle of Fear and Love

Fear whispers "Never dream!"
A death-like visage, icy maw
The hoarder of discarded hope
Devouring all, feigning power
But look, look past the ashen face
To see far greater things than fear
Love
Belief
Desire
The hoarder quails and yields the field
Ah, Love
There is no greater power

9. Representatives of the Nutrition Bureau

"We have a long road ahead of us; we should go."

It was Meyer who spoke up, and Brenton and Joe agreed, so the three loaded up and set off west.

The sun was high, and billowy clouds, riding lazily toward the horizon, dotted a bright blue backdrop. The mood lightened under the bright sky as the companions walked briskly along, when Brenton commented on Mark's absence, saying it felt as though he had been dragging them back on purpose. Joe agreed, and wondered how Mark had made the decision to travel so quickly. Meyer made no comment, changing the subject to ask what Brenton and Joe knew of the Climbers. He was interested in finding out more about them when they reached The Mountain.

It was early afternoon when they reached the eastern edge of the Nutrition Bureau ranch. A fence ran south as far as the eye could see, and another one west with them along the road. Green grass replaced the scrub and clumps of natural brown grasses of the Flatlands. The land had been cleared, and cattle could be seen here and there grazing or resting in the pasturelands. There were occasional water troughs, and small windmills dotted the landscape, pumping the only water to be found in the Flatlands from unseen aquifers.

As they walked they noticed two men, wearing the uniform of the Nutrition Bureau, working on one of the troughs not far from the road. Two horses were tethered nearby. As the travelers passed, one of the men looked up and rose quickly while indicating the friends on the road to his partner. Brenton noticed they were being watched, and an uneasy feeling crept over him. He mentioned it to the others who, after looking toward the men, quickened their pace.

The road dipped, and the men were out of sight when they heard hoof beats approaching the road. The riders appeared at the fence and walked abreast of the companions, their intrusive gaze unwavering.

Brenton spoke quietly to his friends.

"Just keep going. Let's avoid talking to them if we can." He had no idea what to expect, remembering Cara's warnings.

One of the men finally spoke.

"You there, in the green jacket. What are you doing on the road?" He was gruff and terse.

The three stopped and turned toward the riders as Brenton answered.

"We are travelers passing by. We have business down the road." He didn't mention The Mountain, and he remembered the hapless traveler reporting that there was no danger going *east*.

"Are you going to The Mountain?" the man asked. Brenton hesitated, but Joe stepped in.

"What business is it of yours what our destination may be?" he asked, mildly confrontational.

"It is my business to know who travels this road and why," came the stern reply.

Meyer spoke before the others could stop him.

"We are going to The Mountain to visit a friend," he said.

Brenton and Joe tried not to react, and Brenton urged a quiet, stern, "Let's go!"

The three turned away from the horsemen and started walking.

"I advise you to turn back!" The man's voice was rising.

They kept walking.

"I order you, under the authority of Father Bayle and the Nutrition Bureau, to turn back!"

The man was nearly shouting. It was a strange thing to say, and Brenton and Joe looked at each other, walking briskly. *Father Bayle and the Nutrition Bureau?* Brenton was confused. *What authority does he have out here, and why is it connected to the Nutrition Bureau?*

"You are making a grave mistake!" came a warning, but the travelers were undeterred, and kept walking calmly but defiantly west as the riders took off past them in the direction of the farm, with its storage facilities, water towers and dormitories. At first it was a trot, and then they broke into a gallop, the sound of hooves fading in the distance.

"I don't think we've seen the last of them," Brenton said, looking at his friends.

Joe agreed.

"Let's leave the road and walk in the Flatlands to the north," he suggested.

Meyer objected.

"I think we're safe. I don't want to get lost out there," he said, nodding northward. "Cara told us to stay on the road."

Brenton agreed with Joe, however.

"We can stay close enough to the road so we don't get lost."

Just as he finished speaking, a rumble of wheels and clopping of hoofs was heard coming toward them, ending the discussion. As Brenton climbed the high north bank with Joe, he turned to see Meyer hesitantly staring down the road toward the approaching sound, and then he looked up at Brenton and climbed the bank. The three quickly hid behind tall grasses, peering down at the road.

Moments later a wagon pulled by a team of four horses appeared, and two men with high collared grey shirts rode the seat. In the bed were large casks labeled "Nutrition Bureau." The men were chatting as they drove, and soon another wagon with similar cargo came into view, then another. The hidden trio watched in silence as the convoy passed below, and Brenton could see smaller casks between the large ones. They were the small containers that he and Joe had taken the day before. They let the sound of the wagons fade away to the east before standing.

"Let's get back to the road," Meyer suggested immediately.

"No!" Brenton said firmly. "If the horsemen were getting help, they will come along the road."

Joe agreed.

"Let's leave the road. Those men seemed intent on stopping us."

Meyer could make no argument. He was wheezing, so he took out a flask as Brenton wondered again how long they could keep clear water a secret.

They continued west off the road, keeping within a stone's throw of it, traveling slowly over the rough ground. Joe and Brenton ensured that they were keeping course, while Meyer was silent and kept up, and they progressed as well as they could in the raw terrain. They took time for rest, and Brenton and Joe took a gulp of clear water and chewed on the leaves from the morning meal. Meyer made a comment about the bitterness, but Joe and Brenton smiled and remarked on the taste and strength it gave them.

Refreshed, they set out again at an increased pace. The broad, low hill that they had seen that morning rose ahead of them, the road skirting it to the south. Their path took them to the low plateau around the base of the hill, sheer cliffs at its southern edge dropping sharply to the road below. The farm lay just to the south now, with neat rows of crops, field upon field of blue flowers, and the various structures all ominously close.

They were making their way around the hill when they heard the rumble of a wagon, so they moved cautiously to the edge of the plateau. Below them a wagon pulled by two horses was moving east, and in the bed of the wagon three men in field-grey lined each side. Between them lay several swords and two bows, quivers bristling with arrows.

Joe motioned the others back from the rim, but as they pushed away Meyer dislodged a rock, pushing it over the edge. The wagon stopped as the men on the plateau pulled back quickly from cliff's edge, and then moved rapidly west and north around the hill. The north bank above the road was too high to climb for some distance, and they weren't certain they had raised suspicion, but they were taking no chances when they stopped to listen again, only to hear the wagon moving west with them. They rounded the hill and saw one of its spurs continuing west, still steep and high, ending near a fork in the road.

One path branched to the south forming the ranch's western boundary, while the road they had been on turned north, and following its course they saw a "T" where they would find the way west to The Mountain. The north side of the spur dipped into open country which became rougher, with larger rock formations than they had yet seen among low hills and shallow valleys.

Joe motioned them north down the slope, away from the road and the wagon, and toward the "T" that would take them west toward the looming Mountain.

They quickly made their way down the spur, heading across the valley floor toward the intersection, when Joe looked back. Suddenly, without a word, he pushed the others behind some rocks, motioning back the way they had come. Staying hidden, they saw on the crest of the spur six men, all in field-grey uniforms and armed, armed; they were ominous representatives of the Nutrition Bureau.

"I warned you to turn back!" the gruff voice came in a shout from the side of the hill as the men began their descent toward the trio.

"What are we going to do?!" Meyer wheezed in a hoarse whisper. "I should never have come! I should never have come! I don't want to die!"

Joe grabbed his shoulders, shaking him.

"Not now, Meyer!" Joe said forcefully. "We need to think fast."

Brenton was watching the descending force. "They seem pretty confident," he said grimly.

Meyer slumped in a heap and Joe let him be, turning his back on their pursuers, quickly taking in the landscape as Brenton monitored the descent. Some distance away Joe saw a rock formation jutting out of the landscape like a small fortress. The jagged side facing the three looked climbable, and there appeared to be loose rock on it. Joe spoke decisively.

"If we can climb those rocks," he said pointing, "we will at least have high ground. We may be able to use rocks as weapons. I don't see any other way; running won't last."

Joe pulled Meyer to his feet and tried to reassure him, but he was inconsolable and he wheezed heavily, eyes wild, face deathly pale. As terror gripped him, so did symptoms. Brenton was ready to go, snatching quick glances over his shoulder. The relentless hunters were getting ever closer; the three could still get to Joe's fortress rock if they raced.

"I didn't...want to...come," Meyer whimpered, wheezing. "He...made...me...come." His shoulders shook as he sobbed.

Joe and Brenton looked at each other, but there was no time for discussion. At the shocking revelation a thought hit Brenton hard; *Meyer had wanted to stay on the road—he wanted to get back on the road. What if he tries to give us up?* He reached for his flask, and Joe immediately moved to help.

"Drink this!" Brenton shoved the flask in Meyer's face. Meyer mechanically took the flask and a deep swallow, stunning him as the shock of drinking unpolluted water for the first time hit; Joe caught the flask just before it hit the ground. Meyer looked at them, saucer-eyed. His symptoms abated instantly; he had his strength back. He tried to speak but Joe held up a hand.

The other two took a quick drink, Joe stowed the flask, and then crouching low they raced as fast as they could, burdened as they were, to nearby rocks out of sight of the hunters, with Meyer close behind. They

dashed clumsily between rocks, unseen, toward their ultimate destination and then crouching behind the last formation, they paused.

"If they are moving...to where they last saw us...the last dash and
climb...will leave us exposed," Joe panted quietly to his companions.

He lowered his luggage and motioned for the others to do the same.
Joe and Brenton each kept a flask of clear water, and Joe took the only
potential weapon he had: blue poison. Giving the signal, Joe led the
charge, and halfway from their cover to the rock they heard a shrill
whistle. The hunters had reached their original hiding place, fanning
out among the rocks.

The invigorated friends reached the fortress rock and began climbing
out of bowshot, Joe leading, followed by Meyer, and finally Brenton. As
he neared the top, Joe found the final stretch difficult but he struggled
for finger and footholds and pulled himself over the rim. He turned to
help Meyer, then Brenton, as their pursuers united.

The three on the fortress quickly piled rocks. The top was big enough
to find cover from arrows, with rock on each side rising high past the
rim. Joe ran to the back of the rock and was relieved to find that it was
difficult and steep and the sides utterly inaccessible.

The first arrow landed harmlessly. They heard it as it fell out of the
sky, a hopeful shot from distance. Joe picked it up as they took cover.
The head was stained blue; that gave Joe an idea.

"I could squirt poison from the flask if any of them try to climb
up!" Joe exclaimed. He noted that a climber's face would be exposed at
the summit.

They all looked out from cover as two bowmen took up positions to
cover two climbers, while two more grey-shirts circled to the back of the
fortress. Crawling forward, Joe made his way toward the rim which was
angled up enough for him to move without being seen from the ground.
Brenton and Meyer stepped out to throw rocks, missing the bowmen.
Arrows flew back in answer, but the two found cover quickly, while Joe
rolled a large stone over the edge and heard a shout of pain. He dared a
look and saw the first climber slipping clumsily down the rock face. The
second climber avoided his falling comrade as he neared the final push
to the top.

Brenton and Meyer moved to the back, pelting climbers while avoid-
ing blue-tipped arrows. One gave up after a nasty gash on the head. At
the front, hands were reaching for the rim when Joe readied the flask,
and when a mean face came over the edge Joe squirted angry eyes. A
scream, a fall, a thud; the victim writhed in pain, hands to face.

The bowmen tried in vain to get a decent shot while the final climber
at the back gave up under a hail of sharp missiles and rejoined his
compatriots. The three bloodied men regrouped in front of the fortress
and pulled the blinded man away, sending a bowman around to cover
the back.

"You will never escape us!" came the gruff, wounded voice.

The skirmish was won, but the three were trapped as they gathered
arrows for weapons. They looked at each other and smiled; the survival
plan had worked.

They kept an eye on the men nursing wounds below and tried to stay in the middle of the rock out of sight of the bowmen on either side. Concentrating as they were on the front of the rock, they didn't hear or see the three figures slip over the rim that Brenton and Meyer had successfully defended.

"Well done!" came a deep voice just behind them. They jumped, clutching at hearts. A sturdy, handsome man in a light colored vest and pants cropped just below the knee stood smiling at them. He was wearing beautifully made shoes with decorative studs around a triad of pickaxes on the top. Two more men, similarly attired, stood behind him.

"Brenton, Joe and Meyer. I am Carwyn. We are here to help you!"

10. A Tall, Blue Bottle

The Helpers moved the weary trio to the back of the rock. Brenton noticed the archer on the ground, bound and gagged, and pointed him out to the others. The Helpers spoke briefly amongst themselves; they had a plan.

One of them had a bow, and he nocked an arrow, while long-handled pickaxes remained strapped to backs. The companions at the back of the rock moved up to see what would happen as Carwyn stepped forward. The remaining bow on the ground came up just as the second Helper stepped forward with his. In a booming voice Carwyn said,

"We meet again!"

He was smiling down on the men below. The bowman lowered his weapon, the Helper did not, and it was on the hand that held the bent bow that Brenton noticed three names. His attention returned to the men on the ground, now cowering; these opponents knew each other.

"Mr. Astor!" Carwyn continued. "Did I not ask you in the most polite way, just days ago, to cease from attempting to impede travelers along the road west?" He continued to smile; the men below backed away. "I mean you no harm—today—and there need be no further injury. You are free to go, but patience is waning! You may retrieve your comrade from the rear of this rock, and then you may hike your own rears up the hill, back to your lovely farm."

Carwyn's words brought a laugh from the Helpers, and the others on the rock relaxed at the show of confidence.

As instructed, an injured man freed the bowman, bow shattered, arrows gone. The men in bloodied uniforms regrouped and beat a hasty retreat, helping the blinded man along. The Helper with the bow lowered it and turned around. Umit and Constant introduced themselves; Carwyn ensured retreat. As the wounded men began climbing the spur, Carwyn turned.

"Well then," he said, hands on hips. "Shall we?"

Brenton finally drew a deep breath, thinking how much had happened since they first spotted the wagon. He looked at Meyer, whose demeanor was a question.

Joe spoke first. "We need to get our bags."

"Of course," said Carwyn who, like Cara, had a perpetual smile.

Brenton was impatient, questions roiling his mind.

"Why did you wait so long?" The selfishness that he was now so aware of was welling up.

"Are you not proud? We did not want to steal your victory!" The Helpers laughed. Carwyn continued, still smiling. "We were close by. We were ready to engage and poised to do so when we saw that you had won."

Brenton smiled weakly.

Meyer couldn't stand it any longer.

"What did you give me to drink? I've never felt better in my life!"

"We have many things to discuss," said Joe, looking him in the eye. "For now, let this suffice: there is much more going on around us than we have been led to believe, and you have just tasted proof of it."

Meyer agreed to wait, and they climbed down from the rock. As they landed, they looked to the spur as Mr. Astor shouted something. The Helpers all waved, and the others joined in as they all laughed.

They retrieved their bags, readying to move as Carwyn spoke.

"It is mid-afternoon now, and we have a good distance to go to camp. We will move this way," he said, motioning with his hand, "through these rocks, toward the joining of the roads, and there we will pick up the way west, and on to camp."

They moved off west and a little north, angling across the undulating landscape. As they went, Brenton heard something that he had only faint memory of—the Helpers began to sing, harmonizing pleasantly. They were singing about the life of a Helper and the joy it brought them; in some way it reminded Brenton of something from his boyhood. He didn't catch all the words, but it ended:

So carry forth, yes, travel on
Our joy renewed at every dawn
Oh! See The Mountain bathed in sun
A Helper's work is never done

Joe, Brenton and Meyer were smiling and laughing at the sound and urged the singing Helpers on. The group made their way over the low rises and amid the rocks, some larger than the one they had climbed, and eventually came to the intersection. They took the way west and set off toward Lake Yarden as the Helpers called it, and The Mountain. It loomed high above them now, looking more majestic as they moved west.

The companions were relieved to be away from the ranch and its hostile employees. There were questions about their opponents but the Helpers said little, preferring to sing, and there was no complaint. Meyer asked again about the water, but Joe deferred questions until later. During a brief stop for rest and water, Brenton had the idea to offer

Meyer a leaf from the stalk he was carrying, and to his surprise Meyer enjoyed it.

They walked on with light spirits until the sun was setting behind the hills on the far side of The Mountain, beyond Lake Yarden. Carwyn stopped at a place where the land dipped away, ready to lead them off the road, when a cart appeared coming up the road from the lake. The Helpers did not take any action, waiting. The companions looked at each other, confused.

Brenton spoke up.

"Why is that cart from the Nutrition Bureau so near The Mountain?"

Constant replied, "It is not a cart from the Bureau, but that is its destination."

The cart was getting closer when Joe asked, "To whom does it belong?"

"It is a Climber wagon," Carwyn replied as the cart came to a stop beside them.

"Greetings, Climbers!" A heavy-set man wearing a hat with side-pinned brim was driving. Two very old horses were harnessed in front of him. In the bed were large casks without markings.

"Greetings, Duck," replied Carwyn. "You travel late."

"We got a slow start today," Duck replied sighing, and then looking at the three with baggage asked, "Are these Newcomers?"

"Yes, yes they are," affirmed Carwyn.

"Well! Welcome to The Mountain," he said with a broad gesture. "These Climbers will take good care of you! I must be off!"

The Helpers bid him farewell as he snapped reigns, horses straining. Brenton's brow furrowed and he shook his head, looking at Carwyn.

"Why did he call you Climbers?"

"Confusion is found even outside the Village."

Joe had a question.

"What's in the casks?"

"Cargo for the Nutrition Bureau," responded Carwyn. "There is much to learn, all in time." Carwyn moved as he spoke, beckoning them off the road.

They walked north, cresting and descending a hill. On the valley floor they walked west toward The Mountain until they came to a sheer, north-facing cliff. At the base there was a shallow cave, and around the entrance a low rock wall made with piled stones created a courtyard; in its center was a fire pit surrounded with flat rocks arranged like seats.

They unburdened themselves and took some water. Brenton shared some of his with Meyer, while Joe looked on.

"I have to get more of that! Where does it come from?"

"We have yet to discover that," came Joe's reply.

The Helpers lit a fire and moved knowingly around the space, arranging belongings and preparing food. Brenton noticed how they worked together like the first group of Helpers he had met. Sitting around the fire, the Helpers had new delicacies to offer while the companions from Nabal brought out some of their own provisions, not wanting to take advantage of their hosts.

They learned from the Helpers that the closer they got to The Mountain, the more they would become sensitive to any tainted food or water. They all agreed to burn their food, even though Meyer was just beginning to learn that there was something unhealthy about it. The Helpers promised to provide them with all that they needed for the remainder of the journey, assuring them that they would come to journey's end the following day. Hope had risen in their hearts when they met the western road, with The Mountain and glittering Lake Yarden so prominent before them, and now hope grew into certainty, brightening faces.

The moon was rising and the stars shone brightly in the clear sky as the meal ended, and in the gathering dark around them crickets and other insects could be heard welcoming the cool, still night. The Mountain and its cloudy veil watched over the camp like a massive silent sentry.

The group seated themselves comfortably around the fire, ready to address the events of the day. Meyer began, asking after the source of the water. Brenton explained to the Helpers that Meyer had received his first drink of clear water just before the skirmish, and Carwyn said that he knew, but he didn't say how. Joe wanted Meyer to give the reason for his journey, and Meyer agreed that his actions needed explanation.

"We went to visit Father Bayle after the climb, and we had bread and water with him," Meyer began. Carwyn exchanged a glance with the other Helpers. "When we talked to Father Bayle about invitations, he knew that Joe had received one. He knew that Brenton had found something on his porch and had gone to Joe's house before the ascent."

Joe and Brenton looked at each other. Meyer went on.

"Father Bayle knew something about the Ascending Day ceremony, and he thought that you two might be planning a trip to The Mountain. He said he was concerned for you and didn't want you to go. He asked us to trust him, and we both felt like we had to do what he said. He didn't know if you knew where Verdie was, but he suspected you did. He told us where she was, and he told us that if you visited either of us, to tell you we agreed not to go. If you insisted, he wanted us ready to go to try to prevent you from getting there."

He paused, looking at Joe and Brenton.

"Mark was to try to get you to turn back, and turn back himself to try to discourage you. If you didn't turn back, I was to stay with you and find another way to keep you from getting to The Mountain. Before you gave me the water, I was going to give us up."

He paused and lowered his head.

"I didn't know it could be that dangerous on the road."

At this, Brenton was relieved that he had acted decisively, and asked, "Does Father Bayle have that much of a hold on you, Meyer?"

"He has for a long time, and yesterday it seemed much stronger, but I'm sorry for betraying both of you that way." Meyer appeared genuinely contrite.

Joe felt compelled to forgive Meyer, but Brenton couldn't bring himself to it. He had practiced nursing selfish feelings all his life, using them to justify his often-rude behavior. With a clearing mind, he wanted to change, but Meyer would have to earn his forgiveness.

Joe was ready to tell the story of the water. He pulled the invitation out and started to relate the events of the day before. As Joe related the story and how they had come to decide to act, Meyer was even more sorry that he had trusted Father Bayle. The Helpers were amused at the caper, and Carwyn whispered something to Constant.

Joe produced the blue liquid as he related that part of the story, which interested the Helpers. No one had seen how Joe used the solution on Fortress Rock, so he told them; Carwyn wondered aloud if the victim would regain eyesight.

The story of finding the water ended, but the real adventure was just beginning in many ways, and now without a secret between them. Questions turned to the Helpers, and Joe asked the most urgent one.

"Is the source of this water at The Mountain?"

Umit and Constant looked at Carwyn, who answered, speaking slowly.

"You will find what you are looking for at The Mountain. What else you may find, I cannot know."

Brenton thought about Lake Yarden, sparkling in the light of the setting sun. He had been attracted to the lake the day before and assumed it was the source of clear water. Everyone stared at the fire, thinking over what Carwyn had said, when he continued.

"Meyer is not ready to go to The Mountain."

Meyer looked up. "But I want to go! I want more of that water!" he insisted.

"Even so," Carwyn replied, "you are not ready."

Brenton remembered Cara not knowing if Mark and Meyer would respond, and he thought about the difference in the invitations.

He looked at Meyer, who was crestfallen and bewildered.

"Can he still travel with us?" In spite of his lack of forgiveness, Meyer was still a friend.

"Oh yes, of course," Carwyn said, smiling. "All are welcome at The Mountain."

Meyer perked up.

"But he may be a danger to one or both of you. I cannot say for certain." Carwyn's voice was low and soft.

Meyer looked at Brenton, then Joe, and finally back at Carwyn.

"These are my friends," he said. "I've spent much of my life with them. I want more of that water, and I want to be with my friends."

"And yet you allowed yourself to be coerced into a deception in which you were ready to betray them this very day."

Carwyn's voice, though gentle and kind, was firm but without accusation; he was speaking the truth with his charitable smile in a deeply caring way.

It seemed to Brenton that Carwyn dearly wanted to help Meyer, but there was some reason, bigger than all of them, that he could not.

Meyer strained for redemption.

"I'm sorry for my actions," he reiterated, looking at Joe and Brenton. Joe nodded.

"I know that you are," came the gentle reply from Carwyn.

"I was under the influence of Father Bayle, and I had a strange feeling that I should do what he said."

Carwyn thought for a moment.

"You shared bread and water with Father Bayle, yes?"

"Yes...we did," affirmed Meyer hesitantly.

"Was the water poured from a tall, blue bottle?"

"Yes," said Meyer.

"I would advise you never to drink that water again," Carwyn replied.

Meyer nodded, hanging his head. Even after taking healing water he was emotionally exhausted.

Joe and Brenton looked at each other, remembering water from a tall, blue bottle from Father Bayle many times, from the time that he first took them in. It had been a long time since they had visited him, but Mark and Meyer were regular guests in his expansive apartments deep inside Mt. Nabal.

"You should take your rest." Carwyn advised. "Tomorrow you will reach Lake Yarden and The Mountain." He was smiling, happy for the companions and what they might find.

They took his advice and prepared for rest. Brenton kicked off his travel-worn boots, thinking that they wouldn't last much longer. Nearby, Carwyn produced a stringed instrument and began playing quietly. He sang too softly for Brenton to hear all the words, but what he heard made him wonder at the difficult but joyful life that the Helpers led.

The group found places around the fire and settled in for the night, left to think over what they had seen and heard on that eventful day. Brenton fell asleep thinking about Meyer's betrayal, justifying himself for withholding forgiveness.

Nearly two days walk to the east, a bewildered Mark was finding relief in the apartments of Father Bayle, over a loaf and a cup of water from a tall, blue bottle.

On The Value Of Forgiveness

Forgiveness given seems to be
The means to set another free
From guilt or shame they've suffered long
They've yearned to hear redemption's song
But is forgiveness meant to do
A work in them, or work in you?
Withholding it has made you feel
As though your pain is ever real
But can you truly live at all
While ruminating bitter gall?
Forgiveness is a gift you give
That both of you might truly live

11. A Close One by the Fall

The camp stirred at first light under a cloudless sky while an abundance of birds, making a lively but pleasant noise, busily flitted about. Carwyn led the group up to the crest of the green hill above the cliff to take in the sunrise, but instead of facing the sun, they faced The Mountain.

Before the sun touched the group on the hill, it colored the clouds shrouding The Mountain's peak with hues of pink, then gold. It was a wonderful sight to see The Mountain bathed in the sun's first light, and Brenton felt the song from the day before come to life:

> *So carry forth, yes, travel on*
>
> *Our joy renewed at every dawn*
>
> *Oh! See The Mountain bathed in sun*
>
> *A Helper's work is never done*

He hummed what he could remember of the tune, and Constant and Umit gave him an understanding smile as the sun finally warmed their backs and set Lake Yarden dancing and singing a silent, glittering song of its own. They stood in silence, reverent in the presence of the beauty before them.

Smiling at the experience and the prospects of the day, they descended, and the travelers packed as the Helpers prepared the morning meal. Fresh stalks and other plants appeared, seemingly from nowhere. Brenton had not seen the Helpers gathering, and he asked about it.

"We have a saying," offered Carwyn, "'The hand that helps you up has no face.' Brenton, you need no knowledge of the source of this food to enjoy it and be strengthened."

After satisfying drinks of clear water and the food provided by the Helpers, the refreshed and expectant travelers prepared to leave. As he was pulling on boots, Brenton didn't hold out much hope for their survival, wondering where he would find a new pair. Joe and Meyer were in good spirits as they packed, and Brenton realized that the forgiveness that had been asked and given had affected them.

Brenton noticed that the Helpers were in no hurry.

"We are ready to finish our journey," he said to Carwyn.

"Very well," Carwyn responded.

"Aren't you going with us?" asked Brenton.

"No, we have other tasks today," Carwyn said without looking up.

Joe was worried. "How will we cross the lake?"

They had assumed that the Helpers would accompany them on the final stage of their journey.

"Lake Yarden is neither wide nor rough. There are rafts on each side for the crossing. Place your belongings on a raft, remove your shoes and your trousers if you like, and tie rafts together. Push your raft out and swim behind it."

The three looked at one another, and Brenton spoke for all.

"We have never been to a lake," he exclaimed. "We don't know how to swim!"

Umit had been listening nearby.

"Do not lose hope," he said, sensing panic rising. "The lake is shallow, and you can walk far on the shoal. When you can walk no longer, extend your body in the water behind the raft and kick your feet. When you are near the far shore, lower your feet until they find purchase on the rising shoal once again."

Umit finished his instructions, which were clear enough, then he produced a rope and gave it to Joe.

Carwyn had final words for them.

"The land is safe and friendly now, and there is no danger here near The Mountain. Before long the road will take you to lake's edge. Our tasks will soon be completed, and we will return to The Mountain as others take our place, and meet again."

With that he gave each of them a warm embrace, which they received awkwardly. A memory of his parents came to Brenton. They had often embraced him, and he recalled that Verdie had embraced him, crying, before she left. Brenton realized that clear water was healing his mind and his memories—not in a torrent—but in a deliberate, measured way, releasing thoughts in salient moments.

"Farewell! May the road be your friend, and may you find rest at journey's end!" Carwyn had final directions to the road and sent the friends on their way.

They skirted the hill to the west and angled south as directed, found the road with ease, and before long they were walking at a good pace toward Lake Yarden and their first swim. The Mountain loomed large, bright, and bold in the morning sun, rising at the far edge of a verdant plateau. Black cliffs rose above the lake, forming a rounded base for the bright green plain and The Mountain beyond.

As they walked they talked about many things, contrasting the morning before when Mark's arguments and Meyer's silence darkened the mood. They talked about the strange plants they had eaten, the Helpers reserved speech, the possibility of finding the source of clear water, and they talked about Verdie. They didn't know how they would find her, but that did not deter eager steps.

Brenton felt the unspoken barrier between Meyer and him, but they were able to converse cordially enough, and Meyer did not mention the evening before, his actions, or anything about the Village or Father Bayle. He was focused on the road ahead and what they might find at The Mountain, and it appeared to Brenton that Meyer was trying to will his way past the gentle, dark words that Carwyn had spoken the night before.

By mid-morning the three needed a rest from the brisk pace, so they climbed a high point just south of the road to rest and get a better look at what lay ahead. At the top of the small hill they realized how close they were to their goal; Lake Yarden lay just ahead of them. It did not appear intimidating, they agreed, and the sight of it encouraged them all. They took food and drink and once refreshed, descended the hill northwest to the road, picking it up a little farther west than where they had left it. They were excited and energetic as they walked the final distance to the lake with The Mountain, now ominous and beautiful, towering above them in the bright sunshine, its perpetual veil glowing.

It was early afternoon when they descended the last little rise and reached their goal. They passed a small field fenced with wooden poles just before reaching the landing area. Away on either side of them the lake encircled The Mountain and Its round base, with trees at water's edge. Brilliant birds flitted among the trees and over the water, some with long tail feathers that bobbed rhythmically as they flew. On the far side, cliffs rose above them, obscuring the green plane. On the beach directly across they could see two figures waving. A little ways north of the landing beach on the far side a small waterfall came off The Mountain and ran down the beach into the lake. The Mountain, rising at the back of the plateau was black, its cliffs and crags stark above them against the blue sky.

Brenton, eagerly believing that Lake Yarden was the source of clear water, lowered his pack and raced to waters edge where the mild waves lapped against a sandy shore. The others were right behind him as he waded in, giving no thought to boots or trousers. Bending over with anticipation, Brenton scooped water and brought hands to mouth.

The others were in the water with him as he closed his eyes and took it in. Except for that stolen from Mt. Nabal, he had never tasted water without blue solution, but this water wasn't potent. It was clear, to be sure, but it was not the water from the little cask labeled "FB". Though it was refreshing and had an air of healing about it, they had not found the source they were looking for. Disappointed, Brenton retreated to the packs, the others joining him to discuss what they had learned.

"Let's find those rafts and get across," urged Joe. Brenton had lost some of his enthusiasm; he had been sure that Lake Yarden held the secret of the clear water. He got up to help, finding several small rafts pulled up on the bank in the landing area. Soon three rafts were tied together and floating in the shallows with bags, coats and shirts piled high.

They decided to swim with trousers on, but took off their boots and stowed their socks inside. Together they moved out into Lake Yarden.

Soon they were up to their knees, and then thighs were covered. The water was mild, the current was not strong, and the shoal was sandy.

Before long the water was waist deep as they moved slowly, pushing the rafts. Joe suggested they try swimming behind rafts while they could still touch lake bottom, and they all tried it, finding it easier than they had imagined. Brenton remarked that the water made his skin tingle pleasantly; bathing water in the Village had been blue and harsh.

The water was at their chests when they drew close together, the rope floating between rafts. Meyer was on the left, Brenton in the middle and Joe on the right as they shoved out into deeper water, their bodies trailing behind the rafts. They kicked as they had practiced, and before long the little flotilla neared the middle of the lake.

Just past the middle of the swim, Meyer was low in the water when a small wave hit him in the face. He gulped water, choking. Brenton and Joe looked over just as a flustered Meyer let go of the raft with one hand. Unable to regain his grasp, and forgetting to kick as he choked, he began to sink, heavy Village trousers dragging him down. Joe reacted by changing direction, trying to push toward him. Brenton didn't react, a dark thought of revenge clouding his mind. But it quickly passed and he grabbed the rope, took up the slack, and pulled Meyer—one hand barely clinging to his raft—towards him. In the commotion Brenton knocked his weary boots into the water and they were gone. He dropped the rope and reached down for Meyer, grasping his upper arm near the shoulder, pulling up as hard as he could. Meyer felt the helping hand and kicked, and soon he was sputtering and spitting water as his loose hand grasped the raft.

"Are you alright?" shouted Joe.

Meyer couldn't talk, but he nodded, resting a moment, coughing. Soon he nodded again and managed, "I'm OK."

Relieved and wanting to avoid any more mishaps, they started kicking again. What little current there was had moved the swimmers north, away from the landing area, closer to the little fall. The three shoved forward, kicking and splashing. It wasn't long before Joe reached for the lake bottom with a probing toe, then tested again, and found it. All three found the sandy bottom and moved toward the shore. The rise of the shoal soon had them immersed to hips, then knees. Finally they came to the rocks on the far bank near the little stream from the fall.

Pulling rafts onto the rocky beach, they sat to rest. The sun was behind the clouds at the top of The Mountain, moving beyond the hidden peak, but the air was warm. They took off trousers, wrung them out, and put them back on as they took in their surroundings. Meyer wanted a drink, and the little waterfall in the shade of the cliffs looked refreshing.

Brenton was bootless, but the others soon had theirs on, and soon all were picking their way across the rocks and sand. As he crossed a sandy stretch, Brenton noticed marks in the sand; something heavy had been rolled toward the water.

Joe reached the fall first but waited for Meyer to take the first drink. Brenton was right behind them when Meyer did, and he froze, then turned toward Joe and Brenton.

"It's fantastic!" he exclaimed.

Joe and Brenton moved in, not knowing what to expect, filling cupped hands, pulling water to mouths.

Brenton's first drink of clear water back on Mt. Nabal was the best he had ever tasted, but this was better. A similar feeling of wholeness washed over him, but it was deeper, cleaner. He took in more of the cool, clear water falling off The Mountain, feeling connected to it. He thought of Verdie's note and wondered if there was anything more real than what he had found, and that made him think that aside from the water, most of all he wanted to find Verdie.

With their focus on crossing the lake, they had not seen the slender, graceful figure wearing the clothing and gear of a Helper descending the gap in the cliffs just to the south of the landing area. They were so intent on the water at the little fall that they didn't notice the confident person moving down the beach toward them.

"Hello, B," came a sweet, soft voice.

12. Climb With Me

With his mind opened by the water, combined with the ongoing healing and growing wholeness of his body, the soft greeting entered into Brenton's consciousness potent with such hope, love and belief as he had never felt before. He turned, as did the others, and there on the beach stood Verdie. Her eyes sparkled like the lake at dawn, her smile was mischievous and graceful, and Brenton thought he had never seen anyone, or anything, so beautiful. Her blonde, wind-swept hair was cropped short, she was wearing the clothing of a Helper, and she had on beautiful shoes with bright, decorative studs surrounding a triad of pickaxes on the top. She looked strong and healthy, more whole than Brenton could remember, and she had changed into a young woman.

"V!" Brenton was the first to jump forward.

She hugged his neck and he wrapped his arms around her. He had never felt such excitement and joy. He stood back, holding her hands, looked at her, then hugged her again. They were laughing and spinning in circles, her beautiful shoes whirling, floating over the sand.

The others greeted her with hugs, laughing with the embrace. She had been a little sister in the group of friends, and when she left the Village they didn't know where she had gone, or if they would ever see her again. She had been on all their minds since they had first seen the little notes.

"I am so glad you have come!" she said, finally standing back and taking in all three. "I have been watching you since you were on the other side, and I could hardly wait." She looked at Meyer. "Are you quite alright?"

"Yes, I'm fine. Just a scare, nothing more."

She turned to Brenton, saying she was proud of him for helping Meyer the way he did, but he had difficulty accepting any praise. She smiled at Joe, telling him she had missed him and thanked him for helping the friends get to The Mountain.

After the greetings, Verdie suggested that they put their heads under the fall, and they were surprised by the sensation. It made their skin feel alive and invigorated; it felt like healing.

"Shall we be going? You should pull the rafts to the landing area for others to use." She walked with them to the rafts, took off her shoes, and waded next to Brenton.

"Thank you for the invitations, Verdie. Joe and I discovered the clear water, and so much has happened since." It had only been two days.

"We will have time enough for you to tell me your story," she said smiling, happy as ever.

Brenton asked about the water. "Is that fall the source of the clear water?"

She looked at him and smiled.

"That is the fall from the source," she said. "You will see more on the Grand Resting Plane."

"How will we get up there?" Focusing on crossing Lake Yarden, he hadn't considered the cliffs.

"There are ropes affixed past the landing area, " she said.

He nodded, trusting her guidance, looking at the shoes she carried.

"So you've become a Helper?"

"Yes, I am a Helper," she affirmed confidently.

She changed the subject, asking about Mark. Brenton gave a brief account, ending by saying that Father Bayle had influenced Mark.

"I should not be surprised to find that a tall, blue bottle was involved."

At that Brenton looked at her as she continued.

"I stopped drinking that water well before you or Joe. I could sense that it was working ill on my mind."

As they approached the landing area they saw the two men who had waved at them, now seated on rocks, fishing. Behind them, a ways up from the water, there were clothing, boots, climbing harnesses, ropes and flasks laid out on display. The men wore the attire of Climbers.

"Greetings, friends! Welcome to The Mountain. I'm Dale." He indicated Verdie. "You know, you have one of the sweetest little Climbers on The Mountain helping you, " winking at Verdie as he spoke.

The fishermen rose and came toward the travelers.

"I'm Trent. Welcome. Let us know if we can help you," the second man added.

"These are my friends Brenton, Meyer and Joe," Verdie said.

"Newcomers are always welcome," Dale said as he helped them beach rafts. "If you need anything, we have some supplies over there," he said, pointing to the display.

The Climbers had positioned themselves in the landing so that anyone coming across the lake had to pass by them to get to the climbing area to the south, or the fall to the north.

The friends unpacked rafts, and Meyer and Joe pulled on boots and organized their gear. Brenton needed footwear, so he and Verdie went with the Climbers to see what was available.

"Boots are five coins," said Trent. "I'll give you socks with a pair of boots."

Brenton looked at Verdie; he had never had to buy boots before, and he hadn't paid for any of the help or food he had received from the Helpers. He retrieved coins from his bags and returned, handing the coins to Trent who asked,

"Do you need anything else?"

Brenton shook his head.

Trent gave him socks and Brenton began to try on poorly made boots. They were either too small or too large, and then he found a pair that he could wear, but he told Verdie that they were very tight. He laced them, and turned to go.

"Thank you," he heard Verdie say behind him. She joined him on his way back to his bags.

"First Climb is not difficult. Those boots will be fine for now," she assured him.

"They're not a good fit," he replied.

He wished for his old boots, ratty and dilapidated as they had been. Verdie helped him with his luggage, and then led the three past the enterprising Dale and Trent, down the shore toward the climbing area.

"I hope I can buy some shoes like the ones you're wearing," Brenton said, walking next to Verdie.

"This kind cannot be purchased," she replied, turning to smile at him.

Brenton knew by now not to persist with questions.

"There are the ropes," Verdie said, pointing ahead. "This is called First Climb. It would be more aptly described as a very steep walk."

They could now see a gap in the cliffs that looked like a vertical gully cut into the cliff. There were no steps, but the sunken wall had plenty of footholds. Six ropes were affixed side by side at the top and lay down the broad fissure, reaching to the sandy beach.

"Simply step across the rope, take it in your hands, and walk as you pull," Verdie said as she demonstrated, taking several steps up.

It did not look difficult to Brenton, but his boots were bothering him already. The three on the beach took a rope and tested the technique, and the friends managed to move up the steep incline without difficulty. They paused for an occasional rest, Verdie patiently staying with them.

I have found the real water and now I'm climbing with Verdie, Brenton thought as he rose higher.

With a final pull they neared the top, and then all four came out of the gully and on to the Grand Resting Plane.

The Plane spread out before them, an unimaginably verdant carpet of green dotted with flowers and plants of many colors. Fruit trees were everywhere, some arranged in neat orchards, others in roomy groves. White sheep and goats could be seen in small groups, feeding in green pastures. There were birds of all sizes and colors in the air, in the trees, and on the ground, their songs as pleasant as the Plane around them.

In the distance to the south they could make out small buildings in what looked like a little village. To the north they could just see the course of the river that fed the fall. Across the green fields in front of them The Mountain rose, towering over the Plane. Brenton had to tilt his head back to look up toward the clouded peak. Now that he was at The Mountain, it looked both accessible and formidable at the same time.

Paths went out in all three directions. The path before them led across the Plane, and they could barely make out a structure near the first rise of the cliffs.

"We call that part of The Mountain the Lower Reaches." Verdie was pointing just above the Plane. She pointed higher, toward the billowy veil. "The Upper Reaches are just below the clouds." She brought their attention back to the ground. "The camp is just there, at the base."

"What's that village over there?" asked Meyer, pointing down the southward path.

"That is where the Climbers live," she replied.

Meyer said that he would like to go and see it.

"We are going this way," Verdie said pointing straight ahead.

She led them down the path toward the Lower Reaches. As they walked, she picked berries and fruit and passed them along, surprising and refreshing the Newcomers. At one point Verdie stopped and rubbed the top of some grasses in her hands, hulling seeds. She held them up in her hand, and moments later two beautiful little yellow birds with blue wings were in her hand, taking a meal. Finishing, they chirped and flitted away, reminding Brenton of the freedom that his little bird must be enjoying.

Turning his attention back to the path, Brenton remarked about a particularly beautiful blue flower that was ubiquitous on the Plane. It was the same variety that he had seen from the plateau overlooking the Nutrition Bureau ranch.

"Verdie, what are these flowers?" he asked.

"It is Azure Succuro," she responded. "The root has another name. The flower and stem have healing in them. They once covered the Flatlands, but now they are found only on The Mountain."

Brenton was a little confused. "But we saw fields of these at the Nutrition Bureau ranch."

"Yes, they took them from The Mountain, and use them for other purposes." She was silent for a moment, then added,

"Bad things often arise from the perversion or excess of things meant for good."

Brenton thought Verdie wise for her age, and he smiled though she didn't see it. He did not press further, but he thought about the blue liquid he and Joe had found in the little container labeled "Nutrition Bureau." He looked to Joe who nodded slightly.

Verdie was pointing north and west, to the right of the camp ahead as she said, "The pool is over there."

"What is the source for the pool?" Joe was curious.

"The water comes from the rock," she told him. "There is a deep spring that feeds it."

They could not see the pool itself, but Brenton wanted very much to take a drink at the source. His boots were continuing to bother him as they walked, and he longed to put his feet in the healing water.

Verdie greeted a trio of Helpers moving toward the rim, who in turn greeted the Newcomers with smiles and encouragement. The Helpers had packs and pickaxes on their backs, and one had a bow. As they went by, Brenton looked at their hands and saw that they had two names written on them. Before they had gone far they broke into song.

Brenton asked about the climb.

"Verdie, have we climbed with you and found the really Real?"

She allowed the question to hang in the air.

"Did you like the poem?" she finally asked in reply, but didn't wait for an answer. "I am glad you found the clear water, Brenton." Brenton did not insist on an answer to his question, but he had more.

"Why couldn't you just tell us that you had found a source of clear water that could heal us?"

She stopped, and turning to him, touched his arm gently. She looked up at him, remembering, then answered his question.

"You must want to come to The Mountain on your own."

She turned back to the path and kept going.

Brenton thought of Carwyn's warnings about Meyer, and Cara's concerns about the two latecomers, and stole a glance at him. Meyer had heard Verdie's response to Brenton, and his head was lowered as he walked, thinking. They continued on for a time in silence.

As they drew near to the Lower Reaches, coming clearly into view now was a low, broad structure with a thatched roof. Posts supported the corners of the roof, and two more were positioned symmetrically between the corners on all four sides. Round tables could be seen under the structure, and tents of varying sizes and colors surrounded it.

"We are almost there!" Verdie was excited to introduce her friends.

There was activity in and around the space. Children were playing on the green lawns around the tents. Some Helpers were sitting in a circle under a tree, playing a game with a board and stones. Others could be seen at the tables making clothing, shoes, instruments and weapons. Still others were working in preparation for a meal, and all wore light and colorful clothes. There were some Climbers among them, working side by side with the Helpers.

As they passed through the outer tents, Brenton noticed an old man sitting by himself in a low, reclining chair, face to the east. He had grey hair and a short grey beard. His eyes were closed and he was smiling. Verdie took the group to him.

"Uncle Lloyd," she said gently, leaning over and touching his shoulder. The man shook his wizened head lightly, slowly opening his eyes.

"Verdie!" he exclaimed softly, and then he noticed the Newcomers. "Ah, this must be Brenton, Joe and Meyer," he said, rising.

Although he looked old, Brenton could see that he was agile and sturdy. He put a hand on each shoulder, welcoming them to the camp.

"Your journey has brought you far," he said after the greetings, "and you still have far to go." He looked at Verdie, and they smiled at each other. Looking at the Newcomers, he had more to say.

"Young men, I want you to know that I knew your fathers, and they were all good men." He paused, looking at Brenton. "You look exactly like your father." He studied the three friends. "I will see you again at the fire tonight."

He sat down and closed his eyes. Verdie looked at them and smiled.

The newcomers were stunned. None of them had ever met anyone who spoke of their parents. Brenton thought of Joe's words the night they left Nabal: *There is much more going on around us than we have yet discovered.*

On Seeing Beyond The Known

The known, the seen, the comforting
Will always seem the way that's right
For those who trust their eyes alone
Who cannot grasp beyond mere sight
But, oh, for those who dare to dream
Who yearn to feel the breaking day
Spill over planes as yet unknown
They sense their world a different way
And temporal hopes themselves will pale
When dreams of worlds beyond prevail

13. The Invitation to Climb

Verdie took Brenton by the hand as she led the Newcomers around, introducing some of her friends and showing the Newcomers more of the Helper's camp.

"Are there no houses here?" Brenton asked. "We saw houses in the distance when we first climbed to the Plane."

"No, there are no permanent dwellings here. We are on the move much of the time doing our work."

Meyer had a question. "What about the Climbers? Don't they work?"

Verdie paused, thinking of how to reply.

"They have their work, but it is not the same as ours. They would say that it is."

Arriving at a large green tent she said,

"This is your tent. You may stow your belongings."

Brenton didn't think the tent secure, and said so.

Verdie smiled as she told him, "There are no locks among the Helpers, but your belongings are safe."

They went in and dropped their bags. Verdie followed, showing where candles and lanterns were stowed.

"An evening meal will be served shortly but if we hurry I can take you to the pool first."

Moments later the friends were moving quickly to water a short distance away, just to the north of camp. A well-worn path led them to the edge of a beautiful, crystal clear pool. It was round, the edge against the cliff receding under an overhang. The pool was shaped like a large bowl, with a depression in the lip at the eastern edge providing the egress that fed the little river running to the rim of the Plane. In front of them, seven flat white stones lay side-by-side, flush with the ground at the edge of the pool.

"We drink the water together," explained Verdie. "These are called Kneeling Stones."

She walked to a central stone, lowering herself to knees. Although none of them were feeling any symptoms, they craved a drink. She beckoned, and they joined her, kneeling together around her. She looked at each of them, smiled, and stooped to drink with her hands just in front of her. They followed her example, and each took in a drink of the most wonderful water any of the Newcomers had experienced. All of the qualities that Brenton had felt before in the clear water were heightened yet again.

No one said a word, but everyone was smiling at each other as they rose. They were walking back to the camp when Brenton broke the silence.

"It seemed stronger than the water at the fall on the beach."

Verdie smiled as she answered.

"It is stronger. It changes as it moves down The Mountain."

They walked briskly without speaking further, thinking about the water. Just before they reached the camp, Verdie said,

"There will be a ceremony for you tonight." She said no more about it.

The friends all sat together for the evening meal as they once had, inviting some of Verdie's new friends to join them. Dinner was plentiful and delicious, with the mysterious plants, fruit, berries and a small portion of meat. The conversation was lively, and the Newcomers told of their adventures on the road.

Near the table where the group sat Brenton noticed a woman dressed as a Climber and a man in clothing he did not recognize eating with some Helpers. The group was talking excitedly as they ate, and Brenton asked Verdie who they were.

"They are also Newcomers," she told him. "They have both received the invitation and accepted. They begin tomorrow."

Around a fire that evening Verdie's three friends were introduced, and there was a song for the occasion. The chorus of voices was beautiful, and Brenton remembered that his mother often sang to him. The music around him and the water was bringing back memories of her, and he cherished them. Brenton had just come for a visit, but he was feeling at home. After the song, Verdie rose to speak.

"I have invited my friends here for a visit. Two of them have come of their own choosing."

She looked at Meyer and smiled at him. He was trying to smile back, but he was finding it increasingly difficult with every mention of his unworthiness to be at The Mountain. He had drunk the clear water and he wanted more. He liked the Helpers, he liked their food, their music, everything. The only thing he didn't like was the unwelcome assertion that he didn't belong.

Verdie continued. "I would like to thank Aunt Cara, Leila, and Natia for bearing the names of my friends, and for helping them in the Flatlands."

Verdie asked them to stand, to applause. None of the Newcomers had noticed that the Helpers had returned earlier in the evening from their mission. Brenton wondered for a moment if Verdie and Cara were related.

Verdie waited for the Helpers to sit before going on.

"I have sent each of them an invitation, and that is why they have come. Now that my friends are here, I would like to personally invite them to climb with me, as is our custom, with the community as my witness."

The trio had no idea what the ceremony would hold, and this was completely unexpected. Brenton, Joe, and Meyer looked at each other, and then at Verdie.

"Where do you want us to climb with you, Verdie?" Brenton blurted, wondering what the ceremony meant.

"To the Upper Reaches, The Fall on Chasm's Close, and the possibility of complete healing!" she said triumphantly.

All eyes turned to the three dumbfounded friends, stunned faces lit by soft firelight. They had never heard of The Fall on Chasm's Close. They had hoped that the clear water from the pool, as good as it had made them feel, would bring them complete healing, but it had not. Now they were being invited to the possibility of complete healing. *Is it really possible?* thought Brenton. He wanted healing, but he had come here to visit Verdie and to find the source of clear water—not to climb The Mountain.

He looked at Verdie who was glowing. The Helpers around him looked joyful, and the Climber whom Brenton had noticed earlier was smiling through tears.

Like the lash of a whip, the truth struck Brenton for the first time: Verdie was completely healed. He hadn't even thought to ask.

"Complete healing?" It was Joe who spoke first.

"Yes," smiled Verdie, "There is a Fall at a place called Chasm's Close, where the purest water of all heals completely. I cannot say with certainty that all who drink there will be healed, but most are, and I am one of them." She was beaming, anticipating their response to the invitation to climb.

"I will do just about anything for complete healing," Joe said. "And I want it for my friends." He looked at Brenton and Meyer. Joe had come to The Mountain full of hope, and he had expressed it to Brenton. Joe's ideas about the true nature of his world had been challenged long ago, and new ideas found fertile ground. He was ready when he heard the thrilling news.

Brenton stood up.

"I want it too," he said, "but I am not certain that I am ready." He smiled at Verdie. He had many questions, and the suddenness of the news of complete healing had caught him off guard; he needed time to think. Old ideas had only recently crumbled—their foundations were anchored in his mind—and new ideas were still being formed and rooted, needing time to mature.

Meyer didn't speak; he was staring at the ground. The truth was, he didn't belong at The Mountain, and he knew it. The way the Helpers talked so truthfully wounded his pride, but deep inside he knew they were right. What he had always believed to be true had not broken down, and although new ideas had been imposed on him, they had yet to displace the old ones. Although tasting clear water had opened his mind, in spite of how his body felt his ideas were still rooted on Mt. Nabal.

Uncle Lloyd was watching the response to the Invitation to Climb, and spoke.

"I see that young Joe is eager to climb, and Brenton is willing but needs time." He paused and looked at Meyer. "Meyer Brooks is not ready to climb The Mountain, and my heart tells me that he knows this."

It's as if he is looking into my head, thought Meyer. Instead of being instructed and asking advice, he remained silently staring at the ground, and something deep within him decided to feed the resentment that had been growing; self-pity took root in his soul and began to grow into a twisted, noxious weed.

Uncle Lloyd continued. "I have told you that I knew your parents." He looked at the young men solemnly. "Each of your fathers wanted to climb The Mountain, desiring to become Helpers. They planned to move here with their families, and they wanted healing for you."

The friends had only just heard of the possibility of complete healing, and now they were stunned and looked at Uncle Lloyd in disbelief at this new revelation. He stood up as a Helper brought a leather bag to him. He walked over to the three, reached in and pulled out a forest-green jacket. He looked at the collar, and then handed it to Joe. He took out another and handed it to Meyer; Brenton was already wearing his.

"Joe, Meyer. These belonged to your fathers. I sent Brenton his father's jacket a long time ago although I probably should not have. I have kept yours here, hoping that one day I could give them to you." He paused, then added, "Wear them with pride."

He closed the bag, handed it back to the Helper, and sat down.

Many questions had suddenly been raised in the Newcomers' minds. They looked silently at Uncle Lloyd. Verdie walked over to Cara, who handed her a forest-green jacket. She put it on though it was well over-sized, and returned to the three young men.

Hearing about his father's desire created a void of knowledge that Brenton wanted to fill, and he had a brief vision of his parents' faces, but he wanted to have full recall of them. He hoped that the healing water here on the Plane would open locked storehouses of memory. *What would complete healing do to those memories?* he wondered. He thought of the forest-green jacket and Father Bayle's reaction to it, and more questions went wheeling through his mind.

Verdie's voice interrupted his thoughts.

"My father desired to be a Helper, too, as did Mark's. These jackets were gifts to them from a Helper who wanted to see them climb." She looked at Leila and smiled, and Leila smiled back, a tear rolling down her dark cheek. "He was from the Greenlands."

Looking back at the Newcomers, Verdie prepared to close the ceremony.

"I have issued the invitation to climb, and Joe has accepted. Brenton, I will wait to hear your answer. Meyer, I believe that Uncle Lloyd has discerned correctly, though it pains me to say it."

She was looking into Meyer's eyes, and Brenton could see that her pain was real.

"The ceremony is done." She smiled, her lip quivered, and she turned away and sat, face bowed in hands as her shoulders trembled, betraying tears.

Brenton acted on an urge to go to her, putting an arm around her.

The Helpers began a soft song, sung in a round. It was a peaceful sound, and soothing. Questions about the past gave way to thoughts about the future as the Helpers sang about The Mountain and their work. The song ended in unison with a verse that would send everyone away from the gathering with restful thoughts:

> And so we hope, when night is come
>
> That you have found your way back home
>
> To fire and warmth, to kin and friend,
>
> To love and joy at journey's end

The Helpers rose quietly to retire for the evening, and Brenton helped Verdie up, hugging her.

She smiled at him, her cheeks stained.

"I am so sorry about Meyer," she said. "Uncle Lloyd advised me not to send the invitation, but I felt I had too." She sobbed again, then composed herself and smiled. "I should be off to bed. Tomorrow we will talk more."

Brenton took her hand and walked her to the tent shared with Cara, Leila, and Natia. Joe was there, wearing his forest-green jacket, talking with Natia. She was smiling at him the way she had when she commented on his eyes two nights earlier in the Flatlands.

Brenton dared a kiss on Verdie's cheek, and she returned it with a smile. Brenton said goodnight and started for his tent, Joe quickly joining him, grinning.

"It's hard to know where to begin," Joe said, gazing toward the Upper Reaches.

Brenton was silent for a moment.

"Now I know why Father Bayle didn't like my jacket," he said eventually. "It belonged to someone who wanted to become a Helper."

The forest-green jackets and the new knowledge of their fathers raised new questions. The most pressing issue was the potential for healing, but they didn't speak about it as they walked toward rest.

Back at the tent, Meyer was lying on his back, brooding. Brenton was happy to take his boots off; time was not helping them fit any better, and he hoped that he could get different shoes before long.

Joe finally spoke about the ceremony.

"Don't you both want to be healed?" he asked, pleading.

Meyer was silent, his mind still reeling with questions raised by the ceremony and the jacket. "I can't be," he said tersely.

The root of bitterness that he had decided to water with tears of self-pity was growing. *Maybe the Climbers will accept me the way I am.* He had already decided to go exploring away south in the morning.

Brenton paused before he spoke.

"I want healing, Joe, but I'm confused. I came for a visit, not to climb The Mountain. I have to think." *I'm beginning to miss my house,* he thought, *but I want to be with Verdie.* He was taking off his green jacket and as he did, he felt the notice from the Banking Bureau.

"I want you to be healed, Brenton, and I want healing for you, Meyer. I don't understand why they keep saying you're not ready." Joe was almost in tears.

Brenton lay awake thinking, his mind wandering along the path that he had taken since that evening on Mt. Nabal. He drifted into a restless sleep. He dreamt of his parents, and especially his mother. He sat next to her while she read books to him, and he was looking at the pictures as she read. The Mountain towered over pasturelands and farms, gardens and forests, and she told him that he was going to go to The Mountain with her. At that he woke up, wondering if it was a dream or a memory, and he tried to hold on to the pictures with the verdant Flatlands laid out below The Mountain. He slept fitfully the rest of the night, dreaming about his house and The Mountain, Verdie and Mark, the work of Helpers and his job, his father in a forest-green jacket and Father Bayle.

Deep in a dream, Father Bayle stole into Brenton's room, set down a cup and poured water from a tall, blue bottle, picked up a small stack of storybooks, and silently glided away.

14. The Choices of Verdie Brighton

Brenton awoke trying to distinguish memories from dreams. He rolled over, put hands behind head, and stared at the roof of the tent, thinking. He wanted to act, but he didn't know how, because as far back as he could remember he had very few choices to make, and the ones he had made certainly weren't life-changing, or anything close. Dull green pants or dull brown. Grey shirt or pale green.

What if my choices today change my life, and then tomorrow I learn something new that contradicts the decision or makes it a bad one? Brenton thought of Joe's decisive nature, and wondered if he had made his choice in Nabal, intending to never go back. *He'll just tell me what to do if I talk to him. Maybe Verdie can help me, or maybe Uncle Lloyd? Maybe a drink from the pool will help.*

He got dressed and, looking at his ill-fitted boots, decided on bare feet. He poked his head out, surveyed the sleepy camp, and stepped onto dewy grass. The sun hadn't yet risen but small clouds reflected its impending arrival, and the cool morning air filled his lungs, refreshing him as he moved to the trail.

Just before Brenton stepped onto the path, Verdie, who had come out of her tent unseen, snuck up as quietly as she could and slipped her arm into his. Her smile was bright, and she suppressed a laugh.

"Good morning, Verdie!" Brenton said in a whisper.

"It is, yes, and the same to you," she replied. "Shall we get a drink?"

They set off down the path, arm in arm. As they moved away from camp, Brenton asked a question raised the evening before.

"Why is Meyer not ready to be here?" He had been wondering this since his conversations with Cara and Carwyn, and Uncle Lloyd all but made it official; Meyer was not ready to be here, and might even be dangerous. Verdie had sobbed over it, and now she was embarrassed.

"It will not be easy for you to understand," she started, "but I will try." She paused, gathering thoughts. "Only those who are invited may climb The Mountain. No one can do this of his or her own accord, for the consequences are dire. At the Fall, one sits behind it and waits, and sometimes a name, sometimes a vision, or sometimes both, will come to mind. You and Joe received a real invitation from me because Aunt Cara saw your names at the Fall."

She paused again. Brenton had questions but let her continue.

"I wrote the invitations because I knew that you would not know my Aunt if she wrote you. She is my father's sister, and she knew all of you as boys." At this she smiled, her memories long restored.

"So she is your relative?" Brenton asked.

"Yes."

"And Uncle Lloyd?"

She laughed. "No, he is everyone's uncle!" came the reply.

Brenton thought about Cara, and the vision of the blonde woman that he had that morning in the hollow.

"Have I ever seen your Aunt crying?"

Verdie paused before answering.

"All five of us have," she replied softly, looking away across the Plane, east toward Nabal and the brightening sky. She looked back at him and smiled, continuing, "When I was writing to you and Joe, I was so happy for you, but I felt bad for Mark and Meyer, because I love you all like brothers. I asked if I could invite them to visit, and Uncle Lloyd advised me not to, but I pleaded with him and showed him how I would make theirs different."

She stopped walking before she went on. "I was hoping they would both come, just to get away from...from him. I knew they would at least have some healing for their minds, and maybe someone would see their names."

She looked up at The Mountain, then kept going, still holding his arm.

They were at the pool, and Brenton held further questions. They approached the stones, knelt, leaned forward and drank deeply. They were kneeling and holding hands as the anticipated sun broke over the horizon, a golden shimmer spreading over the pool.

Even though Verdie had been healed at the Fall, the water was sweet and good, and cleared her mind with sustaining qualities. Brenton was refreshed, ready to face the decisions before him. They rose and returned, passing others on the path.

"Why didn't you tell us about the Fall on Chasm's Close before last night?" Brenton asked with a hint of irritation.

"For the same reason I could not tell you about the Ascending Day water. You must respond to the invitation by free choice, not by manipulation or coercion. I told you about the Fall and the possibility of complete healing soon after you arrived, but I cannot make you go; you must go because you choose to, and you may still choose to return to Village life."

She lowered her head and looked at the ground, trying to hide a sad expression, but walking there beside her, Nabal was the last thing on Brenton's mind. When they weren't together it seemed an option, but his clearing mind was pushing it farther and farther away.

He had one more question for her, and she laughed when he started.

"Why did Mark and Meyer dislike the leaf from the stalk, but after drinking clear water Meyer thought it good?"

"That is easy," she responded. "The plants that we eat come from high on The Mountain. The drugged mind cannot comprehend the taste. Clear water overcomes this, because it is from The Mountain. They work together, you see?"

"Yes, I think so. How do they stay so fresh?"

At that she put a finger to lips, smiling.

"To learn that secret, you will have to agree to climb with me!"

He let her keep the secret and smiled, saying no more as they walked.

The camp was abuzz as they returned: little ones scurried around them; food and dishes were being set out; and a climbing party was forming. That caught Brenton's imagination, so Verdie took him over.

Among the group he recognized the two Newcomers from the previous evening meal, but they were dressed as Helpers, and they wore beautiful shoes with decorative studs around a triad of pickaxes on the top.

"Where did they get those shoes?" he asked quietly.

"You will see."

"That woman is dressed as a Helper, but I thought she was a Climber."

Verdie smiled as she responded.

"She was invited, as you were. Some come to The Mountain, and for their own reasons, live in the Village. Some are invited to climb, and choose First Climb as fulfillment, staying on the Plane instead of climbing to the Fall. But this woman, who lived in the Village for a time, has chosen to respond to her invitation."

Brenton was confused. "So Climbers don't climb The Mountain?"

Verdie smiled, shaking her head slowly.

Brenton persisted. "Then why do they call themselves Climbers?"

She shrugged, palms and eyebrows raised.

Brenton turned his attention to the climbing party. They were geared to climb and the lead Helper was encouraging them. Brenton overheard him saying that The Mountain was dangerous, and to stay together, but adding that there would be much joy along the way. It was very inspiring, and a twinge of jealousy touched Brenton. He looked up at The Mountain, its eastern face in full sun, and remembering the song he quietly sang the last verse for Verdie, drawing a delighted smile.

Just as he finished someone clapped him on the back, and he turned to see Umit and Constant who greeted him warmly. He returned the greeting, asking about their assignment.

"Today, our work is to climb to the Fall. We helped that man in the Flatlands," Constant said, indicating a Newcomer. "Mr. Astor will not soon forget the encounter!"

Umit and Constant laughed at the memory.

The group was ready to go, and the leader turned and headed toward the trailhead and the Lower Reaches beyond.

"They will sleep on the Minor Resting Plane tonight," said Verdie, but before Brenton could ask what that meant, the leader, who was out ahead of the party, beckoned them on with a cheer.

"To the Upper Reaches, the Fall on Chasm's Close, and the possibility of complete healing!" The words echoed Verdie's words around the fire the night before, and a cheer rose in the camp. A song broke out among the climbing party, and soon all the Helpers in the camp joined in, which touched Brenton deeply. For a moment his desire to climb grew.

After losing the party among the rocks at the trailhead, they turned and went to the shelter where Verdie helped with meal preparations. Brenton noted that Verdie and Joe were much alike in their willingness to help others, and then he saw Joe and Natia helping, Joe proudly wearing his father's jacket.

Brenton looked around for Meyer and not seeing him, excused himself and went in search. He found Meyer in the tent lying on his back, lost in thought. Brenton asked how he was feeling.

"I'm fine, for a person who doesn't belong," Meyer responded, staring sullenly at the roof. Brenton wanted to say more, but said only what he could.

"There is a reason for it all, Meyer," he said, trying to console him.

"There may be," Meyer replied, "but there's no reason to stay only to hear that I'm beyond help."

"Meyer, listen. You are welcome here—we all are. No one has said that you are beyond help, only that you are not ready now."

Meyer was beyond consolation, and Brenton might have had more success talking to a stone. Meyer's heart was growing colder and harder as he shut his mind to anything but hurt feelings. Suddenly he rose, threw some belongings in a pack and readied to leave. Brenton tried without success to reason with him while Meyer grabbed his coat—the one from Nabal—and pushed past Brenton.

"At least eat something!" pleaded Brenton as he followed Meyer toward the eastern path beyond the shelter.

Out for his morning walk, Uncle Lloyd greeted Meyer who kept his head down, eyes averted. Seeing Meyer leaving, Verdie ran after him but Uncle Lloyd held up a hand and she went to him, crying. Stomping down the trail, Meyer did not look back. Brenton went to Uncle Lloyd and Verdie who looked up at them, saying,

"I am so sorry; I chose poorly." She was taking blame for Meyer's actions, but she was only guilty of loving him enough to include him. She left Uncle Lloyd's arms and went to Brenton, trying to see and speak through tears as she had the evening before.

"We will have him back soon. Let us find Joe—," she paused with a smile and took a breath, composing herself, "—and Natia, and take our morning meal."

Brenton took her hand as they turned toward the shelter.

After the meal, Brenton agreed to join Verdie, Natia and Joe in cleanup. Although he generally preferred to keep to himself, he was beginning to enjoy working alongside others and the camaraderie that came with it. While they worked, Brenton asked Verdie about a certain container from which he had seen Helpers drawing a drink.

"Only Helpers who have been to the Fall on Chasm's Close may drink that water," she told him.

After the cleanup, Natia and Joe took packs and left camp heading east, intending to walk the northward trail to the river and perhaps beyond. They were smiling and laughing as they took the path, and Brenton was happy for them and wondered what adventures the Grand Resting Plane held.

Verdie had something she wanted Brenton to see, so she led him by the hand and walked west toward the trailhead, leaving the shelter behind and following in the path of the climbing party. As they chatted she was quick to laugh, the sound stirring Brenton's memories of their time in the apartments of Father Bayle, and faintly, even before that.

Her mood changed as they came nearer the cliffs. She pointed out simple markers just off the trail.

"Those who have gone before lie here," she said reverently. She paused for a moment, looked at Brenton and smiled, and then took his hand and kept going.

Close to the trailhead she stopped, looking up, straining to find something. Brenton joined her, looking up at black cliffs towering over them but at what else he didn't know.

"There they are!" she finally said, excitedly pointing to the cliffs, and soon Brenton saw them too. The climbing party, climbing over steep rocks in their light outfits, stood out against the black backdrop. The lead Helpers moved like mountain goats, the Newcomers following with two more Helpers beside them urging them along. Soon they were over a ledge and out of view as they pushed higher into the Lower Reaches. Brenton remembered his question about the Minor Resting Plane.

"It is a place of rest above the Lower Reaches: a broad mountain meadow covered in green grass, trees and cool water."

"So there is a pool there?"

"Yes, a small one, fed by a fall coming out of a cliff that rises above it, like this," she indicated the cliff wall as Brenton tried to picture the Plane.

As she indicated the cliff, something caught her eye, and she pointed. Emerging from rocks by the lower trail were three figures, two of them Helpers, while the third, wearing the clothing of a Climber, was hobbling with support. Verdie took in the scene in a moment, then quickly began gathering bunches of Azure Succuro as she moved toward the trailhead with Brenton in tow, now doing the same. They reached the trailhead as the three left the trail, the Helpers seeing the flowers.

"Thank you, Verdie!" one said. The Climber, in some pain, was lowered to a flat rock, and one of the Helpers cut a pant leg, gingerly removing boot and sock. He rolled stems and flowers in hands and then pressed the paste gently onto shin and ankle, repeating several times until the lower leg was covered in blue.

"I am sure you have heard the warnings, friend; never climb alone."
The Helper was speaking gently, a hand on the Climber's shoulder.

"I got an invitation...I really did!" the Climber said, the pain in his
leg subsiding as the paste took effect.

"Even so, never climb alone; there are many who would help you."

"I don't have money," the man said sheepishly.

The Helper smiled warmly at him.

"Our payment is sharing the joy of those who find healing."

At this the man lit up. Brenton felt shame. He remembered his
neighbor, old Mr. Parish, whose need he had ignored on many occasions.

"How did he get up there?" Brenton asked Verdie.

"It is common," she replied. "There are many who come here self-
reliant and selfish, not willing to ask for help. Others are simply naïve."

They walked back to camp, leaving the Helpers to care for their charge.

They spent the rest of the day walking and talking, sometimes resting
under a tree. They found plenty to eat, they had much to talk about, and
the day passed quickly. They were not aware of time, and Brenton hardly
noticed his painful boots. They crossed paths with Joe and Natia two
times during the day. The second time both were soaked to the skin and
laughing, and they were holding hands.

Before the evening meal Brenton was starting to feel his once inescapable symptoms, and evening light found them as morning light had,
kneeling side-by-side on polished white stones, drinking from the
mirror-like pool now reflecting pale light and first stars. On the return
walk Verdie stopped, turned to face Brenton and took his hands, looking
up smiling; he waited patiently for her to speak.

"Brenton, remember our talk this morning?" she began.

"Of course."

"I said this morning that I loved you all like brothers. Do you remember the time we spent growing up together?"

"Not as much as I want, but memories are returning."

She paused, looking up toward The Mountain, deciding how
to proceed.

"I loved you as a friend, but more. I was so happy when Aunt Cara
received your name. I wanted very much to see you." She paused again,
looking into his eyes, remembering the Brenton who had not been
affected by water from a tall, blue bottle.

She continued softly.

"Brenton, I have loved you for a long time, and today as much as ever,
even though we were apart."

He was taken aback but smiled even as other thoughts crowded in,
and he wanted to respond with the kind of confidence that she had, but
he couldn't.

"I...I love you...too, Verdie," he managed.

Memories of his parents were faint, and they were the only memory
of love that he had. Expressing it felt awkward because he wasn't sure
when affection for her became love.

They exchanged a brief hug, and he whispered in her ear,

"Thank you, Verdie."

Crowding thoughts returned. He did love her. He loved himself, too, and the comfortable little house on Leeway Street, his locks and keys, his job, his Preservation Reward. Every time something tugged at him to be different, to change or to take a chance, his reaction was retreat—always back to the known and away from the unknown—or just far enough to *feel* different and brave, but not to *be* different and brave; he had another disease as real as the one that enslaved his body.

They walked to camp hand in hand, but between them Brenton had more to think about, life-shaping decisions still ahead.

Verdie Brighton was free. She had chosen to leave Nabal and the clutches of Father Bayle. She had chosen to climb long ago. She had chosen to invite Brenton, and she had made the choice to tell him that she loved him. She wanted him to choose The Mountain, and if he did and if he asked her, she knew that she would choose him.

Dying embers of the amber sun were sinking beyond hills west of The Mountain and the Grand Resting Plane had long been in the gloaming when a lone figure roped up First Climb, onto the southward path; in his pouch, an ornate envelope, sealed with crimson wax.

On The Unknowable Future

Unknown paths, intrepid steps
What draws, what drives desire to act?
How comes the choice to move?
One moment a threshold lies before
The next it rests forever in the past
Does the portal swing but one direction?
Once steps are taken, a course set
What keeps the traveler moving?
Change, inevitable
Future, unknowable
Joy awaiting, or sorrow?
What would inaction cost?
There is but one direction: onward

15. The Choices of Brenton Wilder

The evening meal was a happy occasion, taken with the injured Climber and the Helpers who rescued him. Verdie and Natia were in good spirits, chatting happily about the day, while Brenton caught Joe up on what he had learned.

The injured Climber spoke in a moment of silence.

"Being here is very different from the Climber's Village."

"How is that?" asked Brenton. Meyer had not yet returned, and Brenton was curious about the village.

"The way everyone works together. The laughter. The round tables. Eating together—all of it is different. There are no locks or gates. I like it!"

Everyone smiled in agreement.

"The Climber's village is much the same as the place I left," he volunteered, echoing the traveler that the friends had met on the westward road.

As Brenton helped clean up, he again noticed Helpers drinking from the special container and he wondered at the contents. He put it out of mind and focused on his chores, curious as to where Meyer was. He had been quite bitter as he left, and Brenton worried about his friend and choices he might make. From everything that he had learned so far, Climbers seemed a confused lot, and he hoped that Meyer would return soon.

Verdie, working beside him said, "Thank you for helping."

It was out of character for him, but he had been learning from both Joe and Verdie and somewhere deep inside he felt a change beginning.

With the work done, Verdie took his hand. They made their way to the fire pit.

The Helpers gathered, talking and reflecting on the day. Brenton looked around, taking in the experience of being among such happy and purposeful people. Just days earlier he was living a predictable, controlled existence, but now he was living in community, with open-ended choices ahead of him, and no one was telling him what to do or controlling anything he did. Even Verdie had given him freedom to choose whatever course he wanted, and after the day he had spent with her, he was coming to terms with his choices.

Joe was in good spirits, Natia next to him, and he asked an older Helper what Chasm's Close was like.

The woman smiled.

"It is our custom not to describe it," she said. "You must experience it for yourself."

This answer heightened the mystery of the climb and his desire for adventure, and Joe asked,

"What happens after you are healed?"

Carwyn was sitting nearby with Uncle Lloyd. They looked at each other before Carwyn spoke.

"Joe, if you climb and receive healing, your life will never be the same again."

He paused, gazing at the fire, and somehow far beyond, and then he looked at Joe, smiling.

"As a Helper your greatest joy and purpose in life will be to see others receive what you have been freely given. You will be full of gratitude for what you have received, and your life will center on helping others climb to healing waters. Even if your mission takes you far from The Mountain, your purpose will always be to see others healed. Though you did not know it, you were like a slave to another's will in Nabal. Here, you become like a slave again, but you choose it, and service to the good of others is a light burden to bear."

Brenton, listening in, realized with certainty that if he decided to climb and was healed, his life's course would be set.

Joe had another question. He looked at Uncle Lloyd.

"What if someone drinks at the Fall and turns his back on the life of a Helper?"

Uncle Lloyd thought for a moment before answering.

"It has happened, unfortunately, but only to a very few," he said slowly, staring at the fire. He raised a stern look at Joe as he spoke slowly.

"A disease much worse than the one you have would take you."

Brenton looked at Verdie who had been watching him as Joe was asking questions. She wanted desperately for him to choose to climb. He smiled but said nothing. He was running down the list of objections to climbing in his mind, but the arguments against it were beginning to fade when Joe spoke again.

"I want very much to climb," he said, "and I want my friends to be healed."

A half grin lightened Carwyn's face as he remembered the day he met Joe.

"You are a true leader, Joe. I said so to Constant when you told the story of finding the clear water."

Joe took the compliment with a confident smile.

Brenton was happy for Joe and proud of him. He was now certain that Joe had decided before they left Nabal that he would not go back. When he had talked to Joe about the visit to The Mountain, Joe had said that he was not sure what they would find, but that he had hope. Now Joe had the hope of things yet unseen foremost in his mind.

Carwyn had more to say to Joe.

"Joe, you have the hope of the climb and the desire to help others, but now you need the means to climb. We choose the time for this gift when we believe a Newcomer needs it, and now is your time."

A Helper came forward with a little brown box, handing it to Natia who opened the lid, revealing a beautiful pair of shoes with decorative studs surrounding a triad of pickaxes on the top. There was applause as Joe received his means to climb, and Natia knelt, untying his old boots and removing them. She fitted the new shoes, then sat next to him again.

Brenton was moved by the ceremony.

It was only the evening before that he had learned of the possibility of complete healing, and only days before that had he found clear water. The world that he had known had begun to disintegrate with these discoveries, and his ideas about what was true had been shattered as a result. There was a new reality that he could choose, but he still clung to options.

He could go back to Nabal, as Verdie had said earlier—and he had seen how she reacted as she said it. He could stay among the Helpers, but it would be galling if he didn't climb. He could go with Meyer to the Climber village, but they seemed a contradiction. That choice offered the possibility of visiting Nabal and even keeping his house, but to what end? If he stayed with the Helpers to climb The Mountain, these choices would end, and he would become a different person, but he still wasn't sure that he could give up everything he had known. Verdie sensed that he was deep in thought and put her arm around his.

Uncle Lloyd was telling an old, favorite story, but Brenton wasn't listening; his mind wandered to the container in the shelter. Verdie did not say that it contained water from The Fall; she said that it was only for those who had climbed to Chasm's Close. He wondered what it might contain, and if it might be a way to receive healing without the difficulty of climbing The Mountain.

The story ended, and there was laughter and chatter before Carwyn led the quiet evening song. As the final notes faded into the cool night the Helpers drifted from the warmth of the fire. Brenton and Verdie lingered and Carwyn spoke to them.

"Brenton, you have a decision to make. We will not plan the climb until you have decided what you will do." With that, he left for his tent.

Brenton looked at Verdie and said softly, "I will decide soon."

She smiled at him but didn't reply.

He walked her to her tent and said goodnight and then went to his own. Joe was out on a moonlit walk with Natia, so Brenton was alone as he pulled off his painful boots. He thought about Joe's shoes and wanted a pair, but knew they were only for those with the desire to climb.

He lay on his bedroll, his choices becoming starker as he thought of his home and Village and the comforts they offered. His cleared mind revealed that what he considered comfort was really an acceptance of things as they were; there was no comfort in loneliness, locks, and tainted water. It was freedom from choice that he found comforting because it was safe, but once he had discovered clear water, possibilities and choices that he had never imagined were available.

Lost in thought, he barely noticed when his friend came in.

"Are you asleep?" Joe asked.

"No, just thinking," Brenton replied.

"Have you made a decision yet?" Joe was trying to be patient, but he was anxious to move on to a new life, and spending time with Natia had only heightened his excitement at the prospect.

"Not yet," Brenton replied, "but my choices are getting narrower and my path clearer."

Joe, who had left Nabal with no intent to return, was frustrated with the indecision and had words for Brenton.

"There is no way for you to know this, so as your friend I will tell you. Being around someone as self-centered as you is hard work. In spite of that I have been your friend for a long time." Joe hadn't lit a lantern, so the tent was dark. "Now we have come together to the most important decision we may ever make, and you still insist on your self-centered options. I love you like a brother, and I am asking you to change. Think of someone other than yourself for your own good as much as for those around you, or those you would lead to healing. "

He expected no reply and said nothing further.

Brenton accepted without retort what had been said, knowing that Joe was right—he needed to change. For a time he lay thinking in the quiet darkness of the tent, his mind wandering over possibilities.

Soon Joe was asleep, and Brenton's thoughts turned to the container in the shelter. *What harm would there be in trying a drink from that container?* The idea grew on him, his instinctive desire for safety driving him to seek alternatives to climbing. Thoughts led slowly to action as he quietly pulled himself out of bed, left the tent barefoot, and made his way toward the tempting container.

The moon illuminated the Plane and the tents around him, and scattered clouds glowed in the silvery light. The shelter was dark, but he could see just enough to make out objects in the reflected moonlight. Looking around and seeing no one, he found the container and fumbled for a cup, putting it under the spout and lowering the handle. A trickle of liquid slowly filled the cup. He tried to see what it looked like, but it was too dark. He made his way to the edge of the shelter and held the cup in moonlight. The liquid was clear and pure, tempting him to slowly lift it to his lips. He drank. But unlike the clear water from the pool and even from the little cask on Mt. Nabal, he felt nothing, which confused him. He drank the rest, hoping for something, but the water had no effect.

"No doubt you knew that this water is only for those who have been to The Fall on Chasm's Close."

It was Carwyn! Brenton turned around sheepishly.

Carwyn continued, his tone even and without anger or scolding. "You have discovered that the water will have no effect, because you have yet to drink at The Fall."

Brenton felt ashamed.

"I'm sorry. I shouldn't have taken the water."

"The water is freely offered at The Fall. You cannot steal it, and there is no way to benefit from it except to do the hard work of climbing." Carwyn paused; Brenton stared at the ground. "Sit here and wait for my return." Carwyn indicated a seat and then turned toward nearby tents.

Brenton sat as instructed, thinking about what he had done. Because of his fear he had tried to take a shortcut to healing. He knew now that something in him was desperate for it, but that desire had not fully taken over his thinking, old ideas clinging to his mind like tattered rags in the winds of change. He grasped after them, thinking over his options again, finally eliminating the possibility of ever living in Nabal again. He was committed to The Mountain, and he still had three possibilities.

He looked up to see Carwyn emerge from the tents. With him was Uncle Lloyd, carrying a little brown box. Brenton felt sorry that he had affected the old man's sleep, and he was sure that he would be punished in some way for his theft. The men came over to him and sat down; neither seemed angry.

Uncle Lloyd looked at him. "You are not the first Newcomer to steal water," Uncle Lloyd told him, "and you will not be the last."

"I'm sorry for stealing," Brenton said.

"Yes, I believe that you are. Brenton, this action shows that you seek healing, and yet you have not accepted Verdie's invitation to climb."

He looked down at the box on his lap, then back at Brenton.

"Your father told me something that I have waited to tell you."

He paused; Brenton wanted to hear more.

"Your father wanted to climb The Mountain. He told me about a dream in which he saw you climbing The Mountain, but he was not with you."

Brenton listened silently as Uncle Lloyd finished.

"In his dream you were wearing a pair of these," and with that Uncle Lloyd handed him the little brown box.

Brenton accepted it, slowly opening the lid. Inside was a pair of beautiful shoes with bright silver studs surrounding a triad of pickaxes on the top. Brenton stared at the shoes he had longed for, then at Uncle Lloyd.

"I don't deserve these," he said. "I just stole from you."

"No, you do not deserve them," Uncle Lloyd smiled at him, "and yet without this gift you could never climb to seek healing. You may still choose not to climb, but it cannot be because you were not given the means to do so."

Brenton looked back at the shoes as Uncle Lloyd knelt, lifted the shoes from the box and fitted them on bare feet; they were a perfect fit.

"You have the desire and the means, and now the choice is yours," Uncle Lloyd said, rising.

Carwyn stood and they left Brenton with his thoughts.

Brenton had eliminated the Village as an option, the false comfort of his former life now stark to him. The idea of living at The Mountain among the Climbers without climbing seemed an empty choice. That left only two options, both among the Helpers.

He had a brief vision of himself with the shoes on, high on a black cliff, and wondered if it was anything like the dream his father had. He wanted desperately to be healed, he wanted Verdie almost as much, and now he had the means to climb.

He had chosen to come here on his own. He had chosen to try to steal healing—a wrong choice. The only choice he had left was the one Joe had asked him to make—to think of others before himself. He knew then that the battle in his mind had never been about choosing to climb. It wasn't just his body that needed healing.

Sitting alone and looking out over the verdant moonlit Plane, the last vestiges of old ideas that Brenton held true blew away on a gentle breeze, and ideas that had been planted just days earlier took firm root. He wanted to change, and now he knew how.

On The Wounds Of A Friend

The selfish mind tries to defend
Itself from words, though from a friend
When coddled thoughts are held too dear
Or truth reveals a darkling fear
A bitter root will slowly grow
And given time, entwine the soul
−Wounds felt, a lifeline may reveal
A kiss, a whetted knife conceal

16. The Choices of Meyer Brooks

Brenton rose and stepped out of the shelter, looking down at his shoes, silver studs glinting moonlight. He thought of how he would tell Joe— and he realized that he would not just be telling Verdie—he would be accepting her invitation!

That thought brought out a silly grin. He thought of the climbing riddle, and now he was going to find something Real.

What will it be like?

Excitement was building, just as resolve had on Mt. Nabal.

Brenton returned to his tent, slipped off his perfect shoes and lay down. He slept peacefully, dreaming about sitting on his mother's lap as she sang softly, and he dreamt of his father in his colorful jacket.

As Brenton woke refreshed, Joe was stirring. Brenton, excited to tell him, waited until Joe was fully awake but before he could speak Joe saw the shoes.

"Where did you get those?" he asked, indicating the shoes.

Brenton smiled broadly but said nothing.

"You've decided to climb!" Joe jumped up, hugging him.

"I want to change, Joe. That was the real choice."

"I know," Joe said, smiling.

They needed a drink before the morning meal so they hurried out, talking about their adventure and the future they had chosen. They were returning when they saw Verdie coming toward them, prompting Brenton to run to her and take her hands before she could notice the shoes.

"I accept the invitation!" he blurted out.

Verdie's mouth fell open and she hugged him as she had at the little fall on the beach.

"Oh, Brenton, I wanted so much to hear that." She drew back and looked him in the eyes, hers sparkling with tears, then looked down at the shoes, and finally leaned in and kissed him.

They went back to the pool with her and drank joyfully together. Back at camp news of Brenton's decision began to spread, and everyone congratulated him, fueling his desire for healing. In the tent Meyer's forest-green coat caught his eye, and he remembered the abject self-pity that Meyer was wallowing in and wondered where Meyer was. He put his thoughts aside and went with Joe to help with the meal. Verdie and Natia were already there, Natia hugging Brenton when she saw him.

Verdie beckoned them to a low counter.

"When we climb, we carry no food stores. Food is provided for us."

She took some seeds from a small pouch and drew water from the special container. Setting a seed on the counter, she dripped water on it. In moments it sprouted and grew while the speechless men looked on. Verdie smiled and handed them each a tender, refreshing shoot.

"Where do the seeds come from?" asked Brenton.

"We gather them high on The Mountain. At night they come with the wind from the peak and fall among the rocks."

The mystery was solved, but it was still a wonder, and they watched as the women grew more for the community meal. A variety of seeds yielded plants of different types: some as stalks, some with edible leaves, and some that bore fruit. The aroma filled the shelter.

The morning meal passed, the cleanup was done, and the friends were sitting in the warming sun on a lawn planning the day when Carwyn happened by and broke into the conversation.

"I have some news." All looked at him. "Uncle Lloyd would like to take Last Climb with us."

Verdie and Natia looked excitedly at each other. Brenton and Joe were not certain what that meant, so Verdie tried to explain.

"It is a great honor to go with an older Helper on Last Climb," she explained. "He will share his wisdom with us."

The news only made the prospect of the climb more exciting, Brenton whining playfully about the two-day wait; he had made his decision and he wanted to climb. Carwyn told the group that Leila and Cara would also join the climbing party and then went to begin preparations.

The friends went into the shelter to look through clothing stores. Verdie had just found a vest for Brenton when she looked up and saw Meyer and Duck. They had approached unnoticed and were standing silently on the far side of the shelter near the path. Verdie ran over to greet them, and the others followed.

Meyer didn't smile and he moved sluggishly.

"I am happy to see you, Meyer," Verdie said cheerfully.

She knew where he had been, and she was concerned.

"Nice to see you all," Meyer replied without emotion. "I came to get my things."

Everyone noticed that Meyer did not seem himself.

"Where are you staying?" Brenton had no idea what accommodations Meyer might have found.

"Oh, he's staying with Elder Younger," volunteered Duck, a bit sluggish himself.

At this Verdie and Natia exchanged a concerned look.

"Would you come back here and stay with us?" Verdie asked, concerned that Meyer was spending his time with the Climbers' self-appointed leader.

"No, I can't," he replied. "Elder Younger is giving me work and a place to stay."

His voice was flat and slow.

"Who is Elder Younger?" Joe asked, and Meyer looked at him.

"He is someone who knows all about The Mountain, and he doesn't tell me that I don't belong."

His bitterness was palpable even through his slow speech.

Verdie spoke again, looking Meyer in the eyes.

"You know that Elder Younger has never climbed The Mountain, yes?"

Duck spoke up.

"He knows all about The Mountain, and sometimes we even climb on the rocks near the Village." Duck's eager defense of his mentor was childlike.

Verdie was always gentle with him.

"Yes, I have heard that he leads groups up on to the rocks and low cliffs," she said, smiling at Duck.

She looked back at Meyer. "You really should come back," she pleaded.

Meyer was resolute.

"No, I'll stay in the Climber's village. I need to get my things."

With that he moved past them, Brenton following to the tent.

"At least stay the day. Get a drink of water and rest," Brenton urged.

"I have water from Elder Younger. I have a job to do."

Brenton had seen the look that passed between the Helpers at the name Elder Younger, and concern mounted.

Meyer was packing as Brenton spoke.

"Meyer, I'm worried for you. Please stay with us."

Meyer had no intention of coming back to camp. He had been nursing his rooted bitterness, and Elder Younger had been sympathetic, raising questions in his mind about the Helpers, edging the now befuddled Meyer toward conclusions that he might otherwise have never entertained.

Meyer responded without yielding.

"I'm going with Duck on an errand for Elder Younger. I will return to The Mountain tomorrow evening."

Then Meyer paused, trying to remember something, and gave ground.

"Come to the rim after your evening meal tomorrow. I will listen to what you have to say."

His speech was odd, but the idea sounded good to Brenton who was eager to have another chance to convince him to stay.

Meyer was loaded down and leaving the tent when he stopped and looked at Brenton.

"Maybe you're right," he said sluggishly, still without emotion. "Come by yourself to talk to me."

It was a strange request, but Brenton thought that if anyone had a chance to convince him to come back to camp, it would be him.

Brenton followed Meyer back to the shelter, where Verdie was talking with Duck. She was compassionate, and she always took time for Duck when she saw him. She often invited him to come and live at the camp, believing that he was manipulated at the Village.

Joe and Natia had moved back to the stores, outfitting Joe for the climb, but joined the well wishes for Meyer and Duck as they moved off down the path eastward.

The four returned to their work with much concern expressed for Meyer. Brenton told them of the opportunity to talk to Meyer the next evening, providing at least a modicum of hope.

The rest of the day was spent in preparation. Clothing and equipment were gathered and stowed. Verdie and Natia showed the would-be Helpers knots and gave them climbing advice. The evening fireside was a joyful celebration of Helper life; Brenton and Joe were fitting right in, and they were in very good spirits. After a peaceful nights rest they continued their work. A practice area on cliffs near the pool gave Carwyn an opportunity to train Joe and Brenton on basic techniques. The party anticipated an early start the next morning.

The evening mealtime ended and Brenton reminded the group about his opportunity with Meyer. Joe wanted to go, but Brenton told him of Meyer's stipulation which Joe thought odd. However strange the request, he didn't want to upset Meyer if there was a chance that he might return. Brenton went to his tent, preparing to leave, Verdie following.

"Are you quite certain that you must go alone?" she asked.

"Yes, I should honor his request," Brenton said firmly.

She was concerned for him but she didn't know why.

"May I walk with you a ways?"

Brenton agreed to that and said he would enjoy the company.

Slow moving clouds occasionally darkened the moonlit Plane. The air was cool and carried the sweet scent of flowers. They walked until the shelter and gathering-fire were barely visible behind them, when Verdie stopped.

"I will wait for you here," she assured him.

Brenton thanked her, kissed her cheek and then kept going, quickening his pace, intent on bringing Meyer back.

He was well down the path when a figure appeared, moving quickly toward him. They exchanged a greeting as the Helper moved past him with purpose.

Brenton kept going toward the rim, forming ideas of what to say to Meyer, but as much as he wanted to help Meyer, Brenton was excited about the climb, and he had difficulty thinking what to say as he walked.

Brenton was trying to recall how far it was to the rim and First Climb when he saw a silent, statuesque figure ahead of him. The moon was behind a cloud and he wasn't sure if it was Meyer, so he called out. No reply came, so he slowed his pace. He was getting closer to the person standing at the intersection of the paths, and he called out Meyer's name again. This time a head turned toward Brenton. It was Meyer.

"Hello, Meyer," Brenton said as he approached.

Meyer was standing just off the path.

"Hello, Brenton," he said dryly. "I'm glad you came."

"Where did you go today?" Brenton was curious.

"On an errand for Elder Younger."

Brenton wondered why he would not name the errand, and why he had his baggage with him.

"Will you come back with me to camp?" he asked.

Meyer did not answer immediately, and when he did, he was trying to remember something as he spoke,

"Elder Younger...invites you to...come and vis—"

Meyer's voice cut out as something struck Brenton on the back of the head.

Brenton fell to the ground, unable to move. The sharp blow caught him at the base of the skull, the pain intense. He was face down, unable to hear clearly; there were muffled voices and a brief scuffle, but he couldn't move or see. Rough hands tied his own in front of him, then came a blindfold and gag. He was made to sit up, finding it difficult. He couldn't hear Meyer, and he wondered if Meyer had been gagged. When his head started clearing, two men were talking, and he suddenly recognized the voice from Fortress Rock— *Mr. Astor! How did he get to The Mountain without being seen?*

Brenton was in pain and confused as Mr. Astor hissed in his face,

"I gave you the chance to turn back the first time I saw you in that damned Helper's jacket. Now you'll get what's coming to you, just like your father did—and if you even try to get away, I'll take care of you RIGHT HERE!"

17. The Long Arm of Father Bayle

Brenton froze, mind numb. A crush of emotion and questions overwhelmed him.

What does he have to do with my father? What really happened to him? How does Mr. Astor know who I am?

Brenton was confused, bewildered, and in pain. He had always been told that his father had died from an outbreak in Nabal. He had questions forming that he couldn't hope to have answered.

What do I have coming to me?

Brenton was jerked to his feet, disoriented. He wondered how long Verdie would wait before looking for him. He thought of Joe and the climb. Excitement for the adventure turned to despair.

Someone grabbed his arm and pushed. He stumbled and stayed down as long as he could. His gag was removed, but before he could call out a flask was shoved in his mouth—whatever was draining down his throat tasted horrible. His mind went blank, his thinking clouded, and already disoriented from the blow and the blindfold, he became more confused. Blurry memories of Nabal and Father Bayle came to him, then the pursuit by the Nutrition Bureau.

He was made to stand and move. Dark thoughts swirled, and he tried to fight them. He tried to think of Verdie and Joe and the climb. He groped feebly at these as dark thoughts became overwhelming.

"We're at the edge. You have to climb down!"

His blurry mind suddenly realized that he would have to retreat from the Plane and down First Climb blindfolded! Fear gripped him as one of the men turned him, eased him backward and loosened the rope around his hands. The other was behind him, bracing him. He felt for the edge with a foot. The man behind him positioned Brenton's feet over the rope and handed it to him. Brenton stepped backwards until the rope was taut in his hands. He had climbed up without difficulty but now his heart raced as his mind reeled at the thought of descending into darkness.

"Move!"

It was Mr. Astor again. Brenton slowly lowered himself. He had many different thoughts and emotions trying to find a grip in his swirling, murky head. His survival was foremost, and he tried to focus on his movements.

"Faster!"

The gruff voice was no help. He could think just clearly enough to remember to go as slowly as possible.

"If you don't hurry, you'll get down the fast way. I don't care about orders if it comes down to me or you."

Mr. Astor was anxious to get off The Mountain. He wanted to get back across the lake as quickly as he could.

Brenton had the muddled feeling that whatever had been shoved in his mouth was something much worse than he had ever ingested before, even from a tall, blue bottle. It felt like parts of his brain were turning off, black spots forming in his mind. He tried to move slowly. Fear overcame him as he felt the blackness all around him and growing within.

He began to panic as he felt control of his thoughts slipping from grasp.

— - — - — - —

When Brenton was struck and fell, Meyer was stunned. He had made poor choices since he left camp, but he had no idea that they would lead to this. Elder Younger had asked him to get Brenton away from the camp in the dark, but Meyer didn't know why. He had obeyed blindly.

"Who are you? What are you doing?" Meyer yelled frantically.

"Silence! You did your part. Now leave!"

Meyer was confused and didn't recognize the voice. His mind was murky and his thoughts had been dark, and now his friend was being bound and gagged. The gruff man who had spoken came at him and shoved him away.

He stumbled and fell.

Meyer tried to sort his options, but he was having difficulty. Even in his muddled state he felt dirty and used. There was only one thing to do: he got up, and leaving his bags, ran west toward the Helper's camp.

— - — - — - —

Verdie hadn't been waiting long when she thought she saw Brenton moving quickly toward her.

"Brenton?" she called out hopefully.

"No, it is Gregory. Verdie?"

"Yes," she replied as Gregory emerged from the dark.

"What is it?" She had seen how fast he was moving, and he wanted to keep moving toward camp.

"Walk with me," he said.

She turned, throwing a glance over her shoulder, eyes wide. *Where is Brenton?*

"I was watching on the rim...just before dark when I noticed...something strange."

He was breathing heavily.

"The Climber cart...came down to the corral...but the old horses... were...not...pulling...it. These were big...powerful horses. The two Climbers...got off the cart...and just left the...the two casks...and the horses hitched...with the cart...pointed up the road... Something is wrong... I need...to tell Carwyn."

Verdie had been listening intently as they walked. She stopped abruptly, then turned and began to run east.

"Run and get Carwyn. I am going to the rim!" she shouted over her shoulder.

She remembered the strange feeling she had had about Meyer the day before. She had no idea what she was running toward, but she sensed danger and wished for her bow.

— - — - — - —

Even with his mind darkening and thoughts disjointed, Brenton was doing his best to stall a fuming Mr. Astor.

"Move! I will not hesitate to kill you if I must!"

It was a forceful, gruff whisper, and he was losing his patience.

He looked up at the rim occasionally, anticipating pursuit. He wanted to get back to the wagon and the powerful Nutrition Bureau horses as quickly as possible.

Without warning Brenton began wheezing, and with the gag in place the wheezing was choking him. He was painfully reminded of his need for healing, once and for all. The labored breathing became more intense as he went lower, and it added to his panic.

— - — - — - —

Joe and Natia were sitting around the fire with the Helpers when Gregory came running in off the path. He interrupted a song, asking for Carwyn who got up. The two stepped away from the fire.

Joe and Natia looked at each other. Brenton and Verdie were down that trail, and there seemed to be something important going on. They rose and moved toward Carwyn. Gregory was just finishing his story and Carwyn didn't hesitate.

"Natia! Fetch your weapon! Joe, you stay here!"

Joe was not going to stay, and he ran behind Natia to her tent.

Carwyn called to another Helper, and they quickly disappeared among the tents. Natia grabbed two bows with quivers and handed a set to Joe.

"For Verdie," she said quickly.

They ran outside and were soon joined by Carwyn and the other Helper, David.

"Let us go!" urged Carwyn. "I will explain on the trail."

Gregory was too tired to go with them, so Carwyn left him to explain to the others and urged vigilance. The four set off, running down the trail, Carwyn telling them what he knew.

Joe had worried about Brenton's solitary mission, and he thought about Meyer's strange demeanor the morning before.

— - — — - — - —

Verdie was running down the path when she saw a figure coming west. "Brenton?" she called out desperately.

Before he could answer, she saw that it was Meyer. Meyer stopped and tried to catch his breath as she ran up to him. He was wheezing heavily.

"Where is Brenton?" she asked frantically.

"A...Attacked...we were attacked!"

"What? By who?" She couldn't imagine who it might be.

"I don't know," Meyer answered truthfully.

"Where?! Where is Brenton?!"

"Where the...the paths meet."

He needed water badly.

"Is he hurt?!"

"They tied...and gagged him. I don't know!"

She knew that Gregory would sound the alarm, and she couldn't wait.

"Wait here. Others will come," she said, racing toward the rim.

A sickening feeling began to rise from the pit of her stomach as ideas of whom she might be dealing with began to form.

Meyer sat and rested for a moment. He was trying to think, catch his breath, and control wheezing all at once. He couldn't go back to camp after what he had done, even though Verdie didn't know that his choices had led to Brenton's capture. He had alerted her to the danger, giving him an alibi. He had already eliminated going back to Elder Younger. He needed time to think, and he needed water.

Water!

He remembered the path north to the river, and quickly began making his way back toward the rim.

— - — — - — - —

Although he didn't know it, Brenton was nearing the base of the climb. He had no sense of space or time. His mind was getting blacker, his hopeful thoughts fewer.

Mr. Astor kept looking up at the rim, straining in the changing light to see if there were figures against the sky. He cursed at Brenton and told him to go faster as loudly as he dared. He was getting anxious. He didn't want to defy Father Bayle, but he would if it meant getting away.

He looked up again and thought he saw something. Then he *knew* he saw something.

A solitary figure in bright clothing was at the rim, peering into the black gully.

— - — - — - —

Verdie reached the intersection and saw Meyer's bags. She assumed that whoever had attacked Brenton and Meyer would go down First Climb. She approached the Climb cautiously, but she could not see very far without leaning out over the edge. The gully was black. She stepped back, and noticed movement in one of the ropes. *They are still descending!* she thought as she heard some rock fall. She saw that the first three ropes were moving.

She thought of calling out but knew that would not help; the only weapon she had was the element of surprise. Without thinking of her own safety or what she was in for, she went to the farthest rope and started lowering herself into the darkness.

— - — - — - —

Meyer reached the intersection and picked up his bags. He paused to catch his breath, wheezed heavily, and headed north to the river as fast as he could go.

— - — - — - —

"We're almost down." It was the other man. Mr. Astor had been concentrating on the place where he had seen movement, not noticing that they were about to land.

Brenton's feet, adorned with his beautiful new shoes, touched the ground last, and somehow he decided to stumble to buy time. His mind was reeling, his symptoms worsening.

"Get up!"

Mr. Astor grabbed him.

Brenton resisted as much as he could and got a slap across the face. He stopped trying to think and let himself be pushed down the beach.

— - — - — - —

Verdie kept looking down over her shoulder as she descended. The occasional moonlight was bright on the sandy beach, but the gully was beyond its reach. She was moving quickly—much more quickly than the men below her. She was just past halfway down when she looked again and saw a figure move out of blackness and on to the beach.

Two more figures emerged, one stumbling. She heard a slap. The man on the ground was pulled to his feet and pushed across the beach. He stumbled again and was pulled up roughly.

She kept going as fast as she could without burning her hands.

— - — - — - —

Carwyn and the others reached First Climb, looking for clues, catching their breath. There was no sign of anyone.

"Where is Verdie?" Natia wondered aloud.

Carwyn and David went to the rim. Carwyn looked across the river but couldn't see the cart because of trees on the bank. Then he looked down at the beach and saw dark figures. One man was pushing another who occasionally stumbled. Carwyn stepped back, going to First Climb with David.

Joe had moved to the rim past the gully and was looking down. Natia noticed the movement of just one rope, and then it stopped moving.

Verdie had landed.

Mr. Astor was looking over his shoulder as often as he could. He kept pushing Brenton, who was still resisting, while the other man was moving toward rafts.

Verdie was on the beach. She took one last look up the cliffs, and there against the moonlit clouds, above First Climb, she saw three silhouettes. Another was at the rim, closer to her. She didn't hesitate.

"Down here! They have Brenton!"

They saw her on the beach.

"Joe!" Carwyn shouted. "Let us make haste!"

Natia, Carwyn and David immediately began descending.

Joe had an idea. "Verdie! Your bow! Stand back!"

She looked up and waved in understanding.

Joe readied the bow and quiver, strapping the arrows in, dropped the weapon over the cliff, and then ran to join the others already descending.

Verdie watched for the weapon, scooped it up, and ran down the beach.

Mr. Astor and his accomplice heard the shouts.

So did Brenton, and somewhere in his mind the thought of his friends made him think to stumble.

Mr. Astor made good on his threat and produced a very long knife, putting it to Brenton's throat, drawing it just enough to cut skin.

"Keep moving! Fast!'"

The accomplice had secured a raft and was waiting on the shoal to bind the captive to it.

— - — - — - —

Moving quickly northward, Meyer reached the river. He dropped bags, fell to his knees, and drank deeply. Suddenly his wheezing stopped, he regained strength and his mind cleared.

He stood and, hearing shouts well behind him, went to the rim, looking down. Down the beach to the south he made out three figures moving his way, nearing the landing.

He walked quickly south along the rim. His mind was clearing and a thought struck him: *What have I been drinking?*

He began to remember events with clarity and he was horrified. Shame, no longer masked by whatever had his mind in its grip, overcame him as he walked briskly along the cliff.

Who were the men who attacked Brenton, and where did they come from? he wondered.

He looked across the river, and there in the moonlight he saw the cart with the horses still harnessed to it. *The casks!* He and Duck had brought men to The Mountain. Elder Younger had told them to leave the casks on the cart, the horses harnessed. Duck had objected, but Elder Younger had insisted.

Meyer had chosen badly, and now his friend was in mortal danger.

— - — - — - —

Verdie crouched low as she ran along the beach, moving silently and swiftly. Mr. Astor was the hunted now, and he knew it. He looked over his shoulder but did not see the stealthy Helper as she came within bowshot. She stopped, deciding. The first man, farther down the beach, had waded onto the shoal with a raft. The second was pushing Brenton toward it. For a moment some movement he made, or something about his shape, seemed vaguely familiar.

Ignoring the feeling Verdie picked the man with the raft.

She darted toward the water, then angled north again along waters edge. There was no cover and she was trying to crouch as low as she could, but the man with the raft saw a light-colored blur on the edge of the water moving swiftly toward him.

He shouted to Mr. Astor who turned to look, holding Brenton between himself and the threat, knife pressed to throat.

Verdie quickly dropped to one knee, nocked an arrow and drew back, letting fly. The man at the raft shrieked as the arrow tore into his thigh, lodging in bone. He let go of the raft, hopped and then fell, tugging at the arrow, all the while yelling and screaming.

The commotion shoved the raft away, and the slight current took over.

Mr. Astor could not let go of Brenton to help, and he considered the extreme solution to his growing problem as he backed toward his injured colleague.

Carwyn and his pursuers were well past the midpoint of their descent when they heard the commotion. The engagement had begun; they moved faster.

Up on the cliff, Meyer had made his way toward the landing and could see and hear the scene. He realized that his choices had led to the situation, but he couldn't think of how to redeem himself. His paralyzing self-pity took over. Brenton had refused to forgive him for his complicity with Mark and Father Bayle, and now Brenton's life was in danger.

Meyer gave up all hope of ever talking to him again, let alone asking for forgiveness. His clear mind revealed his double treachery in stark detail and he sank to his knees, weeping. Through his tears he saw a figure draw back and pierce the man at the raft.

Mr. Astor had been close to the raft when his partner was shot. The man was sitting in the water writhing in pain, oblivious to the raft or to the pursuit.

"Get up!" Mr. Astor shouted at him.

The man looked at him, face twisted, and then toward Verdie. She was struggling to remember where she had heard the voice before as she nocked another arrow and looked for her next best shot. The wounded man was too low in the water for her to get a good one in. The other man, the form and the voice beginning to coalesce in suppressed memories, was using Brenton as a shield; she began to cautiously move forward.

"Stay back! I'll slit his throat!"

Verdie froze. Suddenly she recognized him and her cheeks flushed. A horrible memory began to grow in shape and repressed rage began to well up.

She forced the memory down and tried to concentrate on Brenton.

She had seen Mr. Astor's defensive move, but not the knife. She looked intently and saw the knife glinting in the moonlight.

Behind her, Carwyn had led a successful descent and the four were running down the beach toward the action.

Meyer looked on, sobbing uncontrollably at the consequences of poor choices. Carwyn had said he might be a danger and that he didn't belong at The Mountain. Even as he watched the unfolding drama on the beach he was thinking about what he would do next.

Mr. Astor shoved Brenton away and threw the rope to his wounded partner.

"Hold him!" he yelled.

The man took hold of the rope and held it tight, kneeling in the water. Brenton was close to blacking out and his symptoms were killing him. He stood in the water, his knees shaking, his body stooped, his mind limp.

Mr. Astor, trying to make himself small, went up the beach to the rafts and began dragging another to the water. He was so intent on Verdie that he didn't see the figures making their way down the beach along the cliffs.

Natia gave a low whistle which Verdie recognized. She stood, running a few paces forward, her bow at the ready. The full memory of Mr. Astor came back to her, and her intent to save Brenton melded with her growing rage at his captor. Taking an offensive stance, she let fly with fierce determination, willing the flight of the arrow toward Mr. Astor's heart.

Mr. Astor let out a yell and fell to his knees, his right lung pierced. He cursed at her and yelled to his colleague to kill Brenton who was now kneeling in the water, unable to move.

The man was in shock. It took some time for the idea to register and the method to come to mind. He tried to take out a knife from his right side with his left hand while still holding the rope. He had his back to Natia who was moving toward him.

She crouched on the beach and shot. The rope slipped out of the man's hand as he lurched with the impact, falling forward and floating face down, the shaft and feather barely visible near his left shoulder blade.

Mr. Astor tried to get up. Natia and the others were not far from him now.

Verdie ran to Brenton.

Mr. Astor, bleeding from the mouth, saw her and tried to throw his knife at her, or at Brenton, but missed wildly and fell forward.

Verdie picked up the knife, reached Brenton, cut his bonds and tried to pull him up. Brenton had enough perception left to feel her soft hands, and he tried to stand.

Carwyn and the others reached Mr. Astor, Carwyn's pickaxe at the ready as Natia covered him. David approached with his weapon from another angle as Joe ran around them to Brenton.

Verdie and Joe quickly removed Brenton's blindfold and gag.

"Mr. Astor," said Carwyn, "we meet again, and for the last time by the look of it."

Carwyn had cautiously rolled him over with help from David. He was alive, but his eyes were glazed and he was wheezing blood.

Brenton's eyes were adjusting, but he was blinking and wheezing heavily. Joe realized how bad the situation was and thought of the fall.

"Let's get him to water!"

Verdie understood, and the two friends tried guiding him along. Brenton looked around and saw Mr. Astor. His mixed-up mind could not retrieve something very important. He could barely speak, trying to tell Joe to help him to the dying man, but they couldn't understand him.

Brenton tore away and started moving toward Mr. Astor, Joe and Verdie in tow.

He remembered now.

"Somefin...abou...mah...fahzer," he managed through wheezing and numb lips, falling on his knees next to the mortally wounded man. "Wha...happen to...mah fahzer?!"

He was trying to grab Mr. Astor by the collar.

The others looked at each other, questions etched on faces.

Mr. Astor smiled for the last time. He looked at Brenton and feebly reached a hand to Brenton's cheek in a gentle gesture that was completely out of place, a gurgle of foamy blood bubbling with last words.

"Why...don't you...ask...Uncle...L-l-lo..."

The blood rolled down his chin, his features fixed in a smile.

Everyone paused, looking at one another.

Carwyn stepped forward, rolled the dead man over, and slit the back of his high field-grey collar. He pulled the halves apart, exposing a large red tattoo.

"That is no surprise," he said, looking at David.

Natia looked at Verdie who breathed out a sigh of satisfaction and relief.

High above the scene on the beach, Meyer was relieved to see the rescue. At the same time his new reality began to sink in: he did not belong at The Mountain, and he was a danger to his friends. He strained to look east and rued his choices as he acquiesced to the only one he had left.

18. Uncle Lloyd's Last Climb

Carwyn and Joe helped Brenton to his feet. Carwyn looked at Brenton carefully and then exchanged a look with David that Joe did not see. Verdie and Natia noticed.

Brenton stared at Mr. Astor, wondering what secrets he had taken with him. Joe was more concerned with getting Brenton to water as quickly as possible. Verdie and Natia helped get their struggling friend down the beach toward the fall, Carwyn urging them to get to water fast. He and David loaded two bodies on a raft, taking them across the river.

As his friends struggled to help him, Brenton tried to ask about Meyer, and Verdie told him what she knew: the others had not seen him on the path. Joe thought that Brenton was in worse shape than he had been on Mt. Nabal and urged them all on. They were trying to support Brenton on both sides and run as best they could, and soon they reached the fall and helped Brenton to the water. He knelt and drank in mouthfuls and then put his head under the water. The others drank standing over him, their friend safe for the time being.

Brenton felt immediate relief from his symptoms: the wheezing eased and eventually stopped, and his mind cleared slowly. This was a new sensation for him. Clear water had an instant effect on both mind and body, but this time the healing came slowly, and when his wheezing stopped and he could think and talk again, he reported the feeling to Verdie. She smiled and assured him that he would be OK.

With his mind clearing Brenton remembered Mr. Astor's last words.

"What did he say? Did I hear him start to say 'Uncle Lloyd?'"

Joe thought he had heard the same.

Verdie and Natia looked at each other, then back at Brenton.

"Uncle Lloyd will tell you the story. It would not be right for me to tell it. I will only say that Uncle Lloyd knows how our parents died."

Joe and Brenton looked at each other. Brenton was blank and colorless. Joe was puzzled.

"I thought..."

"You thought they died at the Health Bureau," Verdie said. "They did not; let Uncle Lloyd tell you."

Across the lake, Carwyn discovered the empty casks with lids removed, and he and David guessed at the mystery. Carwyn had not approved of Elder Younger's water commerce, but Uncle Lloyd had counseled him not to try to interrupt it; now that would have to change. They loaded the bodies on the cart and Carwyn slapped the horses, sending them running up the hill away from Lake Yarden and back toward the Nutrition Bureau farm.

The party regrouped on the beach. Brenton had regained his strength and his mind was mostly restored, but he could sense his disease even without manifesting symptoms. His lips were numb and that wasn't changing. Carwyn spoke to him.

"Did they make you drink something?"

"How did you know?" Brenton asked slowly.

"I have seen the symptoms before," Carwyn replied.

"Brenton, I must tell you that climbing to the Fall on Chasm's Close is now more important than ever, and we must go with all haste."

Verdie and Natia looked at Brenton, and Verdie came to him and put her arms around him with a look of grave concern.

Joe looked at Carwyn. "Is Brenton going to be alright?"

"He is alright now."

As they came out of First Climb, Carwyn thought he saw a solitary figure standing down the northern path. But the moon disappeared, and he could see no more. At the same time, Verdie had noticed that Meyer's bags were no longer at the intersection. They headed back to camp and each recounted their part in the evening's story. When it had been told from each perspective, everyone wondered what had happened to Meyer.

Verdie picked Azure Succuro as they walked, making a paste for Brenton's head wound and cut. His symptoms returned before they got back to camp, and his friends took him to the pool to drink and fill a flask. Back at camp, Verdie gave Brenton a hug and kissed him good-night, smiling at him with difficulty, her knowledge of the past burdening her thoughts.

Everyone settled in and tried to rest for the climb ahead.

Brenton and Joe were awakened well before sunrise. Carwyn was eager to climb, and he gave Brenton a long look as he woke him. Brenton had been exhausted and did not wake during the night to treat his worsening symptoms. He drank from a flask to ease them and rested a moment. After putting on their new, bright clothes and shoes, Brenton and Joe found Verdie and Natia and they ran to the pool for a drink. They refilled flasks for Brenton and then hurried back to camp.

The climbing party gathered in the shelter and shared a quiet meal. Uncle Lloyd had heard about Brenton's symptoms and he was concerned. Cara was curious about Meyer, but no one knew exactly where he was. All assumed he had gone back to the Climber's village. As they ended the meal there were a few Helpers around the structure, and willing hands helped clean up which allowed the climbing party to make final preparations. Uncle Lloyd went to Joe and Brenton's tent.

"I have much to tell you," he said. "For now I will say that I was present when your parents died, and I helped bury them. They died trying to be healed so that they could bring you here."

Both men were stunned into silence.

Uncle Lloyd put a hand on Brenton's shoulder. "We must go now," he said solemnly. "Your need is great."

He left to gear up, and Brenton and Joe were left with new questions. Brenton's mind was clear and he was fully alert, but the growing awareness of his sickness was disturbing and with it came dark thoughts that he did not wish to entertain. His desire to be healed grew and strained against the weight of the disease, burdening his mind.

Joe could see strain on his face, and he wanted to do whatever he could to help Brenton. Brenton knew that Joe would have taken his pain if he could have.

The whole camp was beginning to stir as they gathered near the shelter, and Helpers and some of their curious Climber guests gathered around. There was a ceremony for Uncle Lloyd, and in spite of the mood at the meal and the concern for Brenton, he was in good spirits, joking about his age and climbing. Carwyn had encouraging words for the group, and he made it clear that speed was of the essence. As he turned to the trailhead, he ended with the ceremonial cheer that Brenton had heard just days earlier:

"To the Upper Reaches, the Fall on Chasm's Close, and the possibility of complete healing!"

They passed the grave markers along the path and Leila stepped aside and knelt near one of them for a moment. She rejoined the group as they reached the trailhead and began making their way up the winding path. The cliffs of the Lower Reaches rose above them, and Brenton wondered how they could seem terrible and beautiful at once.

As they went along he began to feel self-conscious about whatever it was that was afflicting him, thinking that his condition was dampening spirits, so he asked for a song. The Helpers obliged and sang as they walked, their harmonies echoing among the rocks. Joe and Brenton tried to sing along as their companions encouraged them to join in, which soothed Brenton's troubled mind.

They reached the end of the trail and paused on a wide ledge for a rest. The approach had not been difficult, and they were now high above the trailhead.

Brenton looked out over the Grand Resting Plane and the camp well below them. He remembered being on Mt. Nabal, and he shielded his eyes and strained to see it across the Flatlands, dim and barely visible in the distance. The thought of Father Bayle trying so desperately to prevent him from climbing The Mountain came to him, and realizing how close he had come to being dragged off made him shudder. With his friends expressing concern for him, he wondered if he had escaped the threat.

He looked down again and felt dizzy, so he stepped back on the ledge and sat down. He started wheezing, and his mind seemed somehow to tighten. His desire to get up and move fought back, and he winced. Verdie saw him struggling and came over to him with a flask of water from the pool. Uncle Lloyd was watching him.

"Are you feeling dizzy, son?" Uncle Lloyd asked.

Brenton nodded as Verdie looked searchingly at Uncle Lloyd.

The Mountain was bathed in sun as they prepared for the next stage. Their path would take them up a deep, vertical gorge, with The Mountains arms wrapped around them. The cliffs rising on either side limited their views of the Plane to the left and right.

Carwyn's expertise was evident as they went, and everyone helped the Newcomers in the difficult stretches. They took special care with Brenton, and Joe stayed close to him. Uncle Lloyd, climbing like a much younger man, was right behind Carwyn. Seeing Uncle Lloyd climb as he did, Brenton wondered why this would be his last trip up The Mountain. He asked Verdie about it when he got the chance.

"It is his choice," she answered. "Each Helper knows when their time has come to end climbing days."

They climbed all morning and into the afternoon before resting to take a meal.

Brenton needed the rest he got, his dizziness forcing him to stay seated. His thoughts were sometimes disjointed and he tried to force himself to concentrate. Drinking pure water helped. After the meal Carwyn addressed the group, mostly for Joe and Brenton's benefit.

"Above us rise the steepest cliffs of the climb, and above them, our rest on the Minor Resting Plane awaits."

Brenton and Joe looked at each other and smiled. They had struggled through many adventures in the past few days, and now they had struggled high up the Lower Reaches together.

Joe was hopeful. "I'm looking forward to rest and a warm fire."

Brenton agreed, looking up The Mountain to the place where he imagined the little fall and pool that Verdie had described must be.

The group rose and readied themselves for the cliffs ahead. Carwyn reviewed the techniques that he had taught Joe and Brenton the day before, and then they were off, Carwyn in the lead, Uncle Lloyd close behind. Cara and Leila brought up the rear, encouraging Brenton and Joe from below. Natia and Verdie stayed close to them, guiding them up the route, showing them hand and foot holds. Brenton was nervous and excited, and he tried not to look down. Joe was a quick study and encouraged Brenton, as he had most of his life.

Brenton struggled with his mind-numbing affliction, and some of the heights almost got the best of him so he rested often, the others waiting patiently. The going was slow, the cliffs were steep, but Brenton was full of desire.

The light was fading in the shadow of The Mountain with its halo of clouds as he finally pulled himself up the final cliff, over the rim, and onto the Minor Resting Plane.

"Besides seeing you down by the lake, I think this is the most beautiful thing I have ever seen." Brenton was smiling at Verdie through his pain as he spoke, and she blushed.

Before them a broad green meadow opened, surrounded on three sides by gently rising cliffs. The Plane was covered in lush grass and flowers, and fruit trees were scattered about. A small garden grew with plants that Brenton had never seen. Birds sang in the trees and as they flitted around the flowers. Across the meadow Brenton could see the small fall that Verdie had described, the sound of it soft and pleasant.

"It's even better than I imagined," Brenton said, looking at Verdie.

Joe and Natia were already headed for the pool when Brenton took Verdie's hand and followed. The rest of the party moved to a fire pit and began to make camp.

Joe and Natia reached the pool ahead of Brenton and Verdie, lowering themselves onto Kneeling Stones. They drank, and Joe laughed. He didn't say anything to Brenton who knelt with Verdie, waiting for him to make the discovery for himself.

Brenton leaned forward with Verdie and drank deeply, and as they raised their heads, he looked at her. He remembered that she had said that the water changed as it moved down The Mountain, and he smiled as the purest water he had yet tasted coursed through him. A wave of healing touched his wounded mind and tired body, leaving refreshment in its wake. His memory, reawakened on Mt. Nabal, took another step toward healing in spite of the raw awareness of the disease clinging to him, and a clear image of his parent's faces came to mind. It was the best he had felt since his drink from the little fall the night before.

"It's wonderful," he said as Verdie smiled back.

She laughed, delighted at the chance to share the experience with him. She wanted him to be completely healed, and they were moving steadily closer.

"It is fantastic, and it is more pure as we climb," she told him. "That will help you more than you know."

He understood after taking a drink. As his symptoms and dizziness got worse, the water would become stronger until he could be healed.

They rose, and the friends walked across the meadow toward the campsite. Verdie stooped to pick a flower, and as she tucked it into her hair, they all heard a sound and stopped.

"Listen!" Natia was holding up a finger.

There was music in the rocks above them, and when they looked up the low cliffs into the gathering evening, Helpers emerged from the rocks; it was Umit and Constant with the group they had led to The Fall.

There was joy in the meeting of the parties. As the evening meal was arranged, there was talk of the day's climb, and the day's descent. The two Newcomers who had climbed to Chasm's Close were exuberant, but by custom they did not share any details of what they had seen, only expressing their gratitude for the chance to climb. Both had been healed and, behind the Fall, had received names of friends. Now they were Helpers.

Brenton had the realization that besides Verdie, they were the only people he could remember seeing before and after complete healing. He tried to imagine what it would be like to have his mind free, completely clear of the awareness of his disease.

In spite of his condition, the fireside that evening was a delight to Brenton. As expected, Uncle Lloyd told stories about The Mountain and his days as a Helper. Umit had a song to share from his homeland, far from the Flatlands across a sea that Benton had never heard of. As the song ended Brenton asked Umit about his home, and how he had come to The Mountain.

"That is a long story, and one for another day," Umit responded. He turned his head as if he could see something through the darkness, far off in the east.

Leila told the group about her father and his passion for the Helper life, and how he died on The Mountain rescuing a group of Newcomers in a storm. The story was somber but it was more noble than sad. It made everyone think about commitment to the life they had all chosen. The mystery of the green jackets remained unanswered, and when Brenton started to ask about them Verdie silently put an upraised index finger to her lip.

Carwyn told the story of the previous night. Umit and Constant were especially interested. There was an approving, understanding look from the two toward Verdie when they heard that Mr. Astor had died at her hand, and they praised her and Natia for their archery skills. Their own encounters with Mr. Astor in the Flatlands were legendary among Helpers, and now there would be no more.

They both expressed concern for Brenton and encouraged him to be brave. The fire died down and the storytelling ended, and the group sat in contented silence for a while, eventually drifting off to their selected patch of meadow and rest.

The stars were bright above them, and the waning moon cast a pale glow on the Plane and on their faces as Verdie and Brenton lingered by the glowing embers.

"I have dreamed of this climb for a very long time," Verdie said.

Brenton's aching mind, now drenched with the healing from the pool, was filled with waking dreams of his parents.

"I wish that our parents could have climbed The Mountain," he said, staring at red coals.

Verdie didn't look up. "They wanted to," she said.

They didn't say more and soon decided to get some rest, finding some mossy ground near Joe and Natia. The four friends were soon asleep. Brenton's parents visited his dreams unbidden, but not unwelcome.

In the morning Brenton had difficulty getting to water. He was wheezing heavily and struggled to think clearly; the drink at the pool helped considerably.

The two climbing groups ate together before parting. There were glad farewells as the descending Helpers slipped over the rim of the

Plane. Joe and Brenton peered over the edge, watching them for a time, but Brenton became dizzy, so they joined the others in readying for the day. They helped gather some food for the midday meal, then everyone packed up and readied for the climb. Carwyn spoke to Brenton, preparing him for worse symptoms as they climbed higher.

Carwyn and Uncle Lloyd were in the lead, singing as they picked their way up the rocks above the grassy carpet on the way to the Little Resting Plane. Everyone was in good spirits in spite of a gloomy sky and an occasional shower. Brenton needed to stop often. He began wheezing heavily at one point and had a panic attack as his heart and mind raced, but a drink of water from a flask filled at the last pool helped. Brenton and Joe produced their forest-green jackets when the skies opened, and they smiled at Leila when she brought one out. They worked up the rocks all morning, and by noon they had reached the Little Resting Plane.

The Planes became progressively smaller as The Mountain narrowed, but the three-sided cliffs were similar in shape. There was a pooled spring near the cliff that rose at the back of the Plane, and the group padded silently over green grass under laden trees to the Kneeling Stones at its edge. Brenton thrilled at the healing water which eased his aching chest and lungs and soothed his mind. Joe laughed and exclaimed his amazement as his healing continued. All appreciated a rest from morning's climb, and after a good meal they continued.

All afternoon the group climbed from rock to rock, up steep wide fissures, picking their way along a route that Carwyn and Uncle Lloyd knew well. Brenton was impressed with the old man's stamina and his sure movements on the rocks. He hoped that he would be able to climb as nimbly in his old age.

As he climbed, Brenton distracted himself with thoughts of his parents, and he saw their faces more clearly than he had in a long time. He also thought for the first time about what he would do after he descended. As Carwyn had foretold, his symptoms worsened as they rose higher, and he didn't know if it was from the height or the drug. Although he could manage symptoms with a drink, they were returning more quickly after taking water, intensity building.

The Little Resting Plane was far below them, and an ominous headwall rose above them when they reached the Upper Resting Plane. Brenton looked up and wondered how they would overcome the sheer cliff.

The Plane was as luxuriant and green as the Planes below, but it was much smaller. A fall of pure water found rest in a small pool, looking very much like the water on the Minor Resting Plane. Brenton was exhausted, but he made his way to the water with Verdie, and both of them knelt and drank. The healing touch was what he needed, and Brenton moved over to the cliff wall by the pool and sat down with his back to it, resting and reflecting. Verdie joined him, taking a hand in hers. She had nursed him through the day, and worrying for him, she was struggling to keep her own spirits up. The sky had cleared and there was still good daylight as the friends sat together.

"How will we climb the cliff above us?" he asked, a bit confused, remembering that Carwyn had said that the most difficult part of the climb was the approach to the Minor Resting Plane.

"Do not worry, Carwyn will explain." Verdie turned to him and smiled, eagerly anticipating his healing drink at the Fall. She was a Helper and, though seeing anyone drink healing brought joy, seeing a dear friend restored was something that she had anticipated for a long time.

Aunt Cara had cried with joy when Verdie received her first sip of the healing water, and Verdie wondered what her experience might be; she had never seen anyone drink from the Fall exhibiting the symptoms Brenton had.

After resting for a while and taking another drink, the two joined the others at the campsite.

Brenton and Joe watched, still in wonder, as Natia and Verdie poured water from the Fall on seeds they had gathered among the rocks through the day. The aroma from the sprouting plants wafted across the Plane as they ate together, seated in a circle around a small fire. As they ate, Carwyn spoke.

"In the morning we will climb to the headwall, then traverse to the north edge. There is a chimney that must be climbed, then...then we will see the Chasm and the Fall on the Close." A smile broke over his face as he spoke of The Fall.

It was clear to Brenton that the joy of seeing Chasm's Close didn't wear out with time, and he wondered at what he would find. He wheezed heavily now, and the others looked at him with concern, sharing flasks to ease his pain.

After the meal, as the group sat around the fire, Uncle Lloyd brought up Mr. Astor's last, broken words.

"Brenton, your parents carried the same drug in their bodies that you now carry."

Everyone was silent. Joe looked at Brenton, while Verdie stared at the fire. Uncle Lloyd continued slowly, memories of that long-ago night still haunting and fresh.

"We found them in the Flatlands, moving as quickly as they could toward The Mountain, but they had only foul water. We had some clear water, but not enough."

A drug. How did that happen? Brenton thought, but didn't ask.

"We buried them there in the wilderness. One day a friend will take you to see the place." A look came over Uncle Lloyd as if he were remembering something but couldn't quite grasp it, but then it passed as he settled in to staring at the fire.

Everyone was silent until Cara spoke, her voice gentle.

"Your parents left you all with me. My brother told me to be wary of Father Bayle, but I did not have time to ask why."

She paused, moist eyes glinting firelight.

"He came with a group of men and took you from me. After I became a Helper I wanted to rescue you all from him."

Brenton wanted to ask questions, but the time did not seem right. Verdie looked at Brenton, and seeing questioning eyes, she patted his arm in silent assurance that one day all of his questions would be answered.

Cara's last sentence hung in the air, and Brenton imagined a drugged Mark under the influence of Father Bayle, and he thought of Meyer and wondered where he could be.

Away to the east, three day's walk from The Mountain, a very confused and distraught Meyer rode into an eerily dark Nabal on a wagon pulled by four horses carrying casks labeled "Nutrition Bureau."

On Empathy In Loss

I have been to the Valley of Tears
Though I have not walked your valley
I have waded the salt-stream of sorrow
Where did you ford the stream?
I have sat in emptiness and dark
My shade of night was not as yours
I have seen a light shut out, to be lit again on a distant shore
But I do not know the light you saw falter
I have faced the cold world absent the warmth of familiar smiles
And yet I do not know the smiles you remember
Though I have not walked your valley
I have been to the Valley of Tears

19. The Fall on Chasm's Close

Brenton awoke in pale morning light, immediately alert, with the full realization that healing from his disease was possible that day. At the same time, the awareness of his sickness was stronger than ever, and it drove images across his mind of ferocious animals—which he had never seen before—with apparent malicious intent. He had gone to sleep with an image of his parents dying in the wilderness playing on his mind, with their friends around them. The image haunted his dreams and left him wondering if their minds had tortured them before they died.

It felt to Brenton as though the drug intensified any thought that was painful and illuminated any feeling of physical pain so that he became even more aware of it. His clearly functioning mind fought against these drug-induced symptoms. All sorts of memories, triggered by the thought of his parents and stirred by wild brain activity, came to mind.

He remembered now that the families of the five friends who had lived with Father Bayle had been close. He remembered the forest-green jacket that his father wore near the end of his life, and he remembered his mother talking about The Mountain. He had dreamt of these things a few nights before, but now knew them to be memories.

Verdie stirred nearby. He was anxious to talk to her.

Before long she sat up and smiled at Brenton. He waited for her to gather her thoughts, and then indicated the pool, desperate for a drink. The rest of the group was still sleeping as Brenton and Verdie rose and embraced, then moved toward the water.

Brenton spoke softly. "I'm having lots of memories return," he said.

Verdie nodded. "I have waited for your memory to begin healing rather than telling you what to remember."

"Do you have memories of life with your parents?" he asked.

"Oh, yes. I remember everything," she smiled. "You and I have been friends since we were very small."

Brenton smiled and strained to remember as far back as he could. There were images of them playing together, but they were fleeting and incomplete.

They arrived at the pool and knelt to drink as she took a hand, and bracing themselves with the other, they stooped together. For a moment, Brenton's mind was free, soothed by the powerful water. His symptoms abated, and he rested there on his knees with his friend.

As they rose, she looked at him.

"Today, you will drink at the Fall. There are three Kneeling Stones there—we always drink in threes."

She smiled, thinking of the beauty of Chasm's Close that she could never describe. "You may choose who you will drink with."

"I have no idea who to choose," he teased.

He thought of Cara, Natia and Leila and his name on their hands in the Flatlands. He thought of Carwyn and the rescue at Fortress Rock. Then he thought of Uncle Lloyd and the forest-green jacket, and an image of Uncle Lloyd helping bury his parents came to him, and his mind was made up.

In the cool dawn they walked back to the group sleeping on the soft grass and quietly built a small fire together, waiting for others to awake. One by one, the party stirred and rose, exchanging quiet greetings, and gathered around the fire in the misty morning air. It would be an unforgettable day, and the little community on The Mountain was gathered in quiet but excited unity as the sleepiest of the group joined in. Uncle Lloyd made another joke about his age and rising last, and laughter broke out.

Brenton was happy that the severity of his need was not preventing the group from expressing their true nature, as it had for much of the climb. The sun broke over the horizon, and as it touched their resting place, the verdant Plane glowed in the soft, filtered light. Birds awakened by the sun began their work, pouring out songs to the morning, and the peaceful Plane came to life, a vibrant rhythm of vitality underscoring everything. The sun melted away the mist, and soon all felt its full warmth. Brenton rested and tried to relax his mind, still haunted by dark thoughts in stark contrast to the scene around him.

The group of friends shared a morning meal together. The joy and laughter in their conversation matched the natural beauty around them, and everyone's spirits were buoyed by the sound. Leila had a giggling fit at something Uncle Lloyd said, and she laughed so hard she cried. That set the mood for everyone, the jokes and light mood continuing as the group packed.

Brenton needed another drink, wanting to feel well enough to keep up with the mood around him. He wondered how much more he could take of the painful wheezing and mind numbing awareness of decay. His thoughts turned again to his parents, and he longed for the healing that they too had craved for their tortured souls.

He tried to help pack up, and when everything was stowed and loaded, the group set off into the rocks above the Plane with a lively song. The brilliant sunshine added to the feeling of joy that the party felt in anticipation of the day, proximity to the Close acting as a drug of a different kind, driving them all on, with Brenton trying to fit in as best he could.

The climb to the headwall seemed relatively easy to Brenton in spite of his physical challenges, and the communal spirit may have had something to do with it. The cliff above them rose high and flat, with virtually no cracks or holds. It was ominous, but he remembered Carwyn's instructions from the evening before and followed the party in a northward traverse. He had never seen a chimney before, let alone climbed one, and he didn't know what to expect. He would have to pull from a deep well of desire to complete the challenge. The need for healing was now foremost in his mind, the disease itself seeming to war against it.

The group gathered at the base of the chimney. Carwyn had explained how to climb it a few days before, but now he needed to demonstrate. Uncle Lloyd went ahead with Natia as Carwyn gave a few words of instruction and then climbed into the opening, teaching Joe and Brenton as he climbed. Carwyn was a good instructor, and before long the rhythm of hand and foot movements, combined with leverage from their backs, had Brenton and Joe moving up the fissure. The Helpers below shouted encouragement to the climbers as they made their way up. Even as he focused on the work at hand, Brenton wondered what he would experience as he topped out above the chimney.

Partway up the chimney Brenton's symptoms erupted in an explosion of pain and mental anguish. He felt as though his head was in a vice. His thoughts were erratic, panic rising. His mind dredged up images and forced them on him, images of his parents in their last moments, Father Bayle in his many deceits, Mr. Astor and his associates attacking him—it was as though his diseased body was trying to turn his very mind against him.

He fought the mental images with pictures of Verdie, his friend Joe, and his companions around him now, above and below. His body heaved with wheezing, and he craved the healing that was now so close by. His companions on both sides of him sensed his need and did what they could to aid him. Joe urged him on and Verdie, just below him, reminded him that she loved him and wanted him to be healed more than anything. Her deep care for him fueled his desire to climb, and he pushed on.

Joe was above him and reached the top just behind Carwyn. Even in his troubled state Brenton determined to turn his back on Chasm's Close until Verdie was beside him, and he shouted his intentions down to her. She smiled as she climbed and let him know that she had heard him. He wanted to share his first glimpse of it with her, and he pulled himself out of the chimney and on to the ledge above, wheezing and panting, his body aching and his mind straining for control.

He was facing the opposite way from the four who were all silently staring at the Close, Carwyn and Uncle Lloyd with memories of many climbs and the joy of seeing it again, and Joe with his first impressions, Natia holding his hand and smiling beside him.

Verdie emerged from the chimney and joined Brenton, and she helped him move sideways down the top of the headwall, grasping his arm and trying to support him. Brenton looked at Verdie. Her characteristic smile was broad, and she was glowing.

"I'm...ready," he said simply through painful wheezing. She nodded, trying to remember the first time she had emerged from the chimney, and together they turned around.

Across a great Chasm below him lay a beautiful walled garden, carpeted in lush green grass. A Fall at the back of it emptied into a pool. A thrill gripped him. Before he could take it all in, his eyes immediately retreated, trying desperately to find how to get to it. On the garden side of the chimney a white stone stair led down to a paved path, running along the top of a cliff. It curved next to the Chasm, running to a point across from the center of the garden. A half-rounded log lay across the Chasm, bridging the gap. On the far side there was a wall on the very edge of the Chasm and in its center, where the log was seated into the garden, an open arch welcomed all who would enter; there was no gate. Beyond the arch stood a circular table laden with food, a stump at its open center protruding just above table-height. Colorful fruit trees lined the edges of the garden, twelve to a side. Seven flowerbeds broke up the green carpet. One lay in the middle of the garden just beyond the stump, covered in Azure Succuro, and three more on each side filled the garden, filled with variously colored flowers.

A slight depression beyond the central flowerbed could be reached by steps, and in the depression lay a pool of pure water. At the edge of the water, three shining-white Kneeling Stones could be seen, arranged in a semicircle around the curved, lower edge of the pool. The pool receded below a shallow "V" shaped overhang, fed by a Fall coming off the angled plane above. At the back of the plane there was a large, square rock, pouring water from several openings into a pool, which fed the Fall by a narrow channel. Above the rock, The Mountain rose, its mysterious peak hidden from view by the ever-present clouds.

Brenton drew a breath. The scene before him was almost too beautiful to comprehend, and questions flooded his mind as he tried to take it all in. Part of his mind was clear, but he struggled to compose his thoughts as his body and mind fought his will.

"It's...it's...more than I could ever have imagined," he stammered. He looked at Verdie. "I understand...now...why you cannot...describe it."

She smiled and nodded. "Are you ready to drink?" she asked.

The Fall! In his awe at the beauty before him, even through his wheezing, he had forgotten his disease for a moment. Suddenly his desire to drink at the pool was overcome by paralyzing fear that he would not make it across the Chasm. His symptoms were overwhelming him, and he felt the sickness in every part of his body. Standing there, looking at the Fall on Chasm's Close, he had never felt sicker in his life, the proximity of the healing water exacerbating his disease in a way that he could not comprehend.

"I am...ready," he said, "I must...hurry!"

The whole party had emerged from the chimney, and although they had seen it many times before, the sight before them mesmerized all. Carwyn put an arm around Joe's shoulders and looked at Brenton.

"This is a day that you will never forget," he said quietly. He smiled and then remembered Brenton's desperate need. "Come!" He walked to the head of the stair and began to descend.

The group standing on the headwall followed one by one, descending the stair in silence to the path below. Brenton followed Verdie, gingerly descending step by step sideways, his back to the precipice falling away from the stair, the northern Flatlands and hills beyond The Mountain the backdrop. When Verdie reached the path she waited, and then took his hand and they walked side by side, Brenton hugging the inside wall, away from the cliff.

The path was made of smooth, white stone, and Brenton wondered how it had been made. He and Verdie came to the curved corner and turned with the path, following the edge of the Chasm, Verdie at the precipice, Brenton still hugging the wall. Although he was dizzy and gripped with fear, at one point he dared to look down. The Chasm was very deep, and the walls on either side, as well as its floor, were smooth and white like the path. Lying on the floor of the Chasm was a huge iron gate, broken in two.

Carwyn reached the Chasm bridge and allowed Uncle Lloyd to lead. He began to cross with Carwyn right behind him, followed by Joe, then Natia. Brenton and Verdie came to the end of the path and they paused, looking across the Chasm to the welcoming open arch across the bridge. In a bold gentle curve that matched the arch, these words were written:

Whoever will may come

"You go ahead," Verdie whispered.

Trembling, Brenton stepped onto the wooden span that crossed the Chasm. He took one cautious step after another. The "U" shaped Chasm below was open on his right and left, and he felt very small and insignificant against the backdrop of the country that lay out below him on either side.

Verdie followed him slowly, not wanting to press his cautious movements. Uncle Lloyd had reached the far side, and as each person joined him they waited for the rest. Halfway across, Brenton paused. In a desperate, high tone, his voice quivering, he said,

"I can't go on!"

Verdie, three steps behind, was in tears.

Brenton had never experienced vertigo before, but now he had a desperate desire to hurl himself from the bridge. Something lurking in a dark corner of his mind urged him to do it.

His right foot was ahead of his left, his body slightly turned. He looked down into the Chasm, and then beyond, to the hills behind The Mountain and the southern Flatlands. He leaned forward.

"Lean back!" Verdie whispered desperately behind him, and he did, then got his feet side by side and faced the open arch.

He slowly, feebly, painfully lowered himself to hands and knees. He wanted so desperately to run down The Mountain and lie flat in the middle of a vast desert.

Verdie leaned carefully forward, speaking softly. "Brenton, I love you, and I know you can do it."

In spite of his condition, Brenton heard her. He remembered the moment on the beach when his mind was so clear and she had surprised him with a soft greeting. He reached deep for the feeling of love, hope and belief that he had in that moment, and it drove him to start to crawl across the narrow traverse.

Verdie, Leila and Cara waited for him to move farther ahead, remembering the first time they had crossed. He continued with more gentle reassurance from Verdie. Slowly, deliberately, he crawled, the four ahead of him watching his progress nervously; it was all any of them could do. The three behind him took cautious steps so as not to rush him, and they were helpless, too. He was wheezing, his mind was reeling, but he kept going, thinking of the healing just before him, and the woman just behind him. He was looking down at the log and straining forward when helping hands gently took him under the arms and then quickly pulled him off the bridge, through the open arch, and on to the luscious grass. He lay flat on his belly, his face in the grass, his arms outstretched above his head.

"I...made...it!" he wheezed. He lay there, resting as best he could, waiting for healing.

Everyone waited just inside the garden and as Cara arrived, without a word they all took off their shoes. Brenton was helped up to join the group, pulling off his own beautiful shoes.

Stepping-stones led around either side of the laden table with the stump in the center, leading to the small stair before the pool. Brenton looked at the stump, then back at the bridge. He had many questions to ask, but he knew that in time they would be answered.

Carwyn spoke to the group. "You may each choose two companions to drink with," he said, smiling broadly.

Joe took Natia's hand and asked Carwyn to drink with him.

Verdie had told Brenton about the ceremony and he had already made his decision.

"I...would...like...to...share...this...moment...with...Verdie...and... and...Uncle Lloyd," Brenton said through his wheezing. He doubled over, wincing.

The most important thing on everyone's mind was getting Brenton to water. Usually there would be laughter and lightness of heart as Natia led a dash to the water, laughing as she glided over the stepping-stones, but this time at the Close she quietly helped get Brenton to the only thing that could save him. As they half dragged the wheezing, wincing Brenton to the pool, Uncle Lloyd, who was supporting him on one side, spoke.

"Before you drink, try to settle your mind and concentrate your thoughts on something that you love. This drug will fight for control of you, and you must hang on to that thought until the healing can cover you."

Brenton nodded as they helped him down the steps. He was aware of everything around him, but the closer he got to the water, the stronger the dreadful grip on his mind became.

"I wanted...you to go...first, Joe," Brenton managed, "but I... am losing...control..."

Joe understood, and told Brenton that he appreciated what that meant.

Verdie led Brenton to water's edge.

"Thank you for climbing with me," she whispered in his ear. She wanted to smile and cry at the same time, having anticipated this moment for so long, but not at all in the way that it had played out.

The three knelt, Brenton in the middle, and he managed a look to either side of him. He was ready, and he was desperate. He remembered what Uncle Lloyd had told him, and with the free part of his mind he grasped at the moment that he had seen Verdie on the beach with all the mental strength he could muster.

They bent to drink, and as they did the same presence that had urged Brenton off the bridge screamed at him to stop. He paused, trying to discover who it was, or what it was, and then tried to push the impulse away as he grasped at the image of Verdie again. The others were taking in the water as he continued down and drank. He expected a wave of healing to come over him, but in place of the feeling he wanted so desperately, a stabbing pain shot through him.

A heinous shriek built up somewhere within, bursting over Brenton's consciousness in a bizarre combination of sorrow, horror, and pain. It shocked and terrified him and his stunned mind went blank. The others watched helplessly as he lurched forward, face first, into the glistening crystal pool.

20. Whispers Beyond The Plume

Uncle Lloyd had been prepared. As soon as Brenton passed out, he grabbed the back of Brenton's vest at the neck and pulled back. Verdie helped him, and Carwyn and Joe, ready to drink as they were, rushed in. They pulled Brenton out of the pool and laid him gently on his back. The group gathered around him and stood silently as Verdie lay beside him on the grass, leaning over him, soft tears falling gently onto motionless cheeks.

Brenton's mind became active before his eyes opened. The first thing that his healed mind became aware of was a feeling of perfect love. The image of Verdie that he had grasped at passed over his mind, then Joe was laughing, and then he was on his mother's lap, and she was singing softly. Whatever had gripped his mind, whatever had been slowly driving him mad, was gone; no more fear, no vice grip.

His clear mind searched over his entire body for any sign of the disease that had enslaved him his whole life, the sickness that his wounded mind had illuminated more and more as he climbed.

It was gone.

There was no trace of it. He had a moment when he thought that he had died, and he was in some place where disease did not exist, a place with no fear, and no more tears, a place where only love exists. His mind was so clear, and his disease so completely gone, that he could not imagine that he was still alive.

Then he remembered the beauty of Chasm's Close, and he thought of Verdie without him in the beautiful garden, and he tried to wake from the lucid dream.

He wiggled his fingers, feeling the deep grass. He heard a soft gasp, and knew it was Verdie. He opened his eyes.

The first sight that his healed mind took in was Verdie, bright eyes dripping tears, smiling down at him. She was bent over him, looking intently into his face, desperate for more movement.

He smiled back.

He did not notice the rest of the group gathered around looking down on him until they all laughed.

He closed his eyes again, still smiling. A peaceful joy gripped him, as he knew that in that moment, on that Mountaintop, his disease had been conquered.

Suddenly he jumped to his feet, and before anyone could react, he began running in circles, leaping as he shouted for joy.

"I am HEALED!" he shouted.

His friends laughed and whooped.

He collapsed on the grass sobbing, tears of joy drenching the perfect green grass. Verdie came to him, putting arms around him, laying her head on his back. She who had been healed long before was just as joyful as he, sharing grateful tears. She let him control his emotions before she whispered in his ear.

"Joe has not taken a drink yet," she said softly, patiently.

In all of the emotion and healing awareness, he had lost his realization of the situation around him, not noticing that his friend had not been healed.

Brenton sat up and looked at Joe. Natia, standing behind him, had arms around his chest, peering over his shoulder; they were both smiling at him.

He rose and went to Joe, leaving Verdie on the grass.

"I'm sorry, Joe," he said, "I wasn't thinking..."

Joe just smiled.

"I'm so happy for you," he said as he hugged Brenton.

Joe had said more than once that he wanted healing for his friends, and he had seen his desire partly fulfilled in Brenton's healing; now it was his turn.

Joe took Natia by the hand, and Carwyn joined them as they knelt. Joe looked at both of them and then led the ceremony by stooping first. They all took in a deep drink and then raised heads from the water. Joe threw his head back and took in a deep breath, then broke into laughter. Everyone cheered and clapped as the three rose to their feet.

Natia hugged Joe, and Carwyn slapped him on the back. Looking at Joe, Brenton thought that he was actually glowing and that Joe had never looked younger or healthier. Joe hugged Brenton again, and the two friends were beaming and laughing as the others went to drink.

Cara and Leila invited Uncle Lloyd back to the pool with them. The three of them drank together as the others looked on. They rose from the water, and as they did, spontaneous joy overtook the entire group. Cara jumped into the water, followed immediately by Uncle Lloyd. Everyone else joined in, splashing and laughing as the healing waters covered their bodies. It wasn't long before the idea of taking off outer garments seemed to strike everyone at once. The water seemed to invite innocence and abandon, and they reveled in the soothing touch of the water on their skin.

For a time they settled into the water, letting the purity of it soak in. They were silent and smiling, faces to the sun. After a period of reverent silence Verdie spoke to Brenton.

"You may now go through the Fall and sit on the other side, beneath the overhang. Close your eyes and wait. You may receive a name, or a vision, like a whisper in your mind."

Brenton nodded. Cara was smiling at him, and he remembered that it was she who had received his name. He smiled back as he moved toward the Fall.

He stood under it for a moment, The Fall pouring a healing shower over his head; it sprayed out gently in a beautiful, soft plume all around him.

He moved beyond it, noticing where the water slipped into the rock wall at the base of the overhang. He sat in the shallow water behind the Fall, eyes closed, not sure what to expect.

He tried to clear his mind. His memories were being restored, and he had a good deal to think about, but there behind the Fall he stilled his thoughts, listening in quiet anticipation for whatever might come to him.

He didn't have long to wait:

MEYER

It was as clear as anything he had ever seen or thought about. He didn't see a face, just the name. He wondered briefly where Meyer was at that moment.

That thought faded as another name came to mind:

PARISH

Mr. Parish? A twinge of shame touched him briefly, and then it was gone, erased by healing water. *How will Mr. Parish climb?* He let go of that thought quickly.

He tried to clear his mind again, and waited.

He had been so manipulated by whatever Mr. Astor had forced him to swallow that he had almost forgotten what it was like to have control over his own mind.

He sat patiently, not wanting to leave this place of quiet and peace.

Without warning a violent thud broke over his mind at the same instant as a scene of a man wielding a sledgehammer pounding brick; it was he! He was wearing his forest-green jacket, but it had some patches or insignia on the shoulders and over the heart. Verdie was next to him, similarly attired, but now her jacket fit. She had a hefty hammer, too, and together they were demolishing a building.

The image faded, and a new image slowly emerged.

In the scene there was a white house...and farm buildings...all were surrounded by gardens and pasture...and there, in the background, The Mountain rose, towering, beautiful, inviting. Verdie sat on a porch smiling down at little children playing around her feet. In the slowly expanding vision, Brenton realized that the house was situated in the Flatlands, and then he saw other houses and farms. A small watercourse wended its way through the scene.

The images gradually faded, and he sat for a while, contemplating, waiting to see what might come next. He saw his parents clearly in his mind, but it wasn't a vision; it was a memory. He knew somehow that he needed to talk to Father Bayle, but the thought was not fearful.

He waited a while longer. He was at peace and his mind was clear, but nothing more came to him so he moved slowly back to the group in the pool and sat quietly, thinking.

He looked at Verdie and smiled, thinking of the scene with the sledgehammers and green jackets, and he wondered what the whispers could mean.

The group took their turns behind The Fall, emerging with a mixture of emotions.

Verdie emerged obviously suppressing a laugh, girly giggles slipping through hands held to mouth, trying not to break up the quiet scene.

Uncle Lloyd returned with a somber smile, and Brenton wasn't sure if the moisture on his cheek was a tear. As he waded past Brenton he leaned over and said,

"There is something very important I must tell you—I can hardly believe that I forgot about it." He patted Brenton's shoulder and smiled.

Leila came back looking hopeful and a bit restless, craning her head from side to side and trying to look over her shoulders at something distant that she imagined back west, beyond The Fall, the overhang, and the shrouded Mountain peak.

Joe and Natia both emerged with glowing smiles. Joe sat with a confident look, arms folded, and when Natia returned she went straight to him, putting her arms around his neck, leaning her forehead on his.

Carwyn looked sad but resolute, then he smiled briefly and glanced at Cara who did not notice the look.

Cara for her part emerged looking a bit puzzled but smiling, and it was then that she met Carwyn's eyes, and blushed.

No one was speaking, the mood reverent. When everyone had taken their time behind The Fall, they got out of the water and put their dried clothes back on.

Carwyn led the group back to the round table at the entrance. Brenton had been thinking so much about his vision that he didn't realize how hungry he had become. He ate eagerly, the food tasting better than anything he had ever had.

He asked Verdie where it came from.

"It is always here when we arrive." She smiled.

He remembered Carwyn's saying back at the cave beneath the rock face and decided to just enjoy the meal. He turned the conversation back to The Fall.

"Verdie, did you get a name?" He asked.

"Yes, I did! But I will not say who it was," She said, teasing him. "Did you?"

"Yes," he said, smiling. "I will play you at your own game."

She laughed. "Did you have a vision?"

"Yes," he said. Then he added softly, "More than one."

For a moment he stopped short of sharing more with her, unsure of how she might interpret what he had to say, then he ventured to tell just a small part of what he had seen.

"I saw the Flatlands, green and beautiful, with houses and farms," he said, studying her face for any clues.

She smiled, a far-away look in her eye.

"Yes, that is how they once were."

He thought of the pictures in his storybooks and remembered how the Flatlands had been depicted. He stopped himself from saying what he was thinking.

But my vision was of the future, not the past.

"Was there more?" she asked, seeing in his eyes that he hadn't shared all.

"Let me think before I say more," he responded.

A moment later he remembered that there was one thing that he did need to tell her.

"I need to go back to Nabal," he said slowly, "to ask Father Bayle about our parents."

She looked at him, and even in that beautiful garden, there was a hint of fear in her eyes.

"But...but are you not afraid?" she asked.

"Not anymore," he said, smiling confidently.

He couldn't yet know what the whispers beyond the plume had meant, but he was sure of two things, and whatever else happened he wasn't afraid: he was finally and completely healed, and he had a future with Verdie Brighton.

On Drawing Strength From Memories Of Those Passed

No flowers grow, no signs of life
To give away the barest thought
That once, what was in silence laid
Beneath a mound, or verdant sod
Had then been vibrant, sentient clay
But knowing and remembering
A dear ones face, a voice in song
A peaceful presence fills the place
A calming peace
That makes hearts strong

21. The Way Through the Wilderness

The sun passed behind the clouds at the top of The Mountain and emerged again below them before the group began preparations to leave Chasm's Close and the restoring Fall.

After eating, they had rested under the colorful fruit trees or wandered around the garden, speaking quietly. Brenton had never had a more restful day. He and Verdie had sat on the bank with bare feet in the healing water, talking about the life of a Helper.

When they were ready to go, they all filled flasks at the pool, and Carwyn filled a larger container to help replenish the supply back at camp.

Brenton smiled as he slipped his feet into his beautiful shoes. He had finally found a pair that fit, and they looked like they would last forever.

As the group prepared to leave, on the inside of the arch Brenton noticed these words:

Chosen to Climb

He remembered the invitation juxtaposed on the outside of the arch, and wondered at the apparent contradiction.

He had no trouble negotiating the bridge over the Chasm as fear had left him completely, and he approached the challenge with a smile. The group climbed the stair and then paused at the top of the headwall for one last look at the Close.

Uncle Lloyd knew that he would never see it again, and tears lined his cheeks as he smiled, remembering his long history with the beautiful garden. Brenton looked at him and thought that rather than looking sad, he had a glimmer of hope in his eye.

Before they left the headwall, Leila pointed south and west to mountains in the distance, telling Brenton and Joe that her country lay just beyond.

In spite of the tears from Uncle Lloyd, the descent to the Upper Resting Plane was light and joyful. Carwyn was in a mood for a song, and he taught Joe and Brenton the old song that they had first heard in the Flatlands:

The Mountain paths are rough and steep
And dangers lurk in fissures deep
But we are fitted for the climb
To drink in hope the Fall sublime

The healing Fall is sweet and clear
The mended body need not fear
The sickness, or its icy hold
For Helper's hearts are brave and bold

We travel not as some we see
Enslaved, unable to break free
Their names we hope to see or hear
To help them break the bonds of fear

We travel light, our spirits glow
With love and friendship, both we know
From hearts fulfilled and bodies strong
From voices lifted full in song

We help the seeker find their way
We see them safe at end of day
To Planes of rest and meadows sweet
To rest refreshing and complete

We will not cease from helping those
Who in this Mountain seek repose
We help the weary scale the heights
To see them drink its Fall's delights

So carry forth, yes, travel on
Our joy renewed at every dawn
Oh! See The Mountain bathed in sun
A Helper's work is never done

They took their time coming down The Mountain, and over the next four days passed two groups ascending. When the climbing groups met there was laughter and a song or two. Brenton and Joe shouted encouragement to the Newcomers as they ascended. They were Helpers now, and they began to take their new role of encouraging others to heart.

Brenton did not speak of the visions that he had seen at the Fall, but he did share with the group that he had seen Meyer's name, and he told them about Mr. Parish. No one knew where Meyer was, but everyone was glad that he would now have the choice to respond to the Invitation to Climb. Joe had received Mark's name, and the friends wondered how he would respond to an invitation. Verdie was delighted that she had received Duck's name. She had not actually received a name; she had seen a vision of a duck, but she discerned what it meant.

They reached the Helper camp in the early evening on the fourth day of the descent. They enjoyed a good meal together and then gathered with the others around the fire where Uncle Lloyd told the story of his Last Climb, embellishing here and there for dramatic effect. The story of Brenton's healing needed no embellishment, and everyone clapped when it was over. Anyone was free to reveal his or her invitees, and all were glad to hear that Meyer's name had been received. A Climber who had just joined the group remembered Meyer, but he had not seen him recently. A Helper trio recently in the Flatlands had seen a lone traveler heading east, dressed like a Villager from Nabal. Brenton thought that it must have been Meyer, but why he would be heading back toward Nabal remained a mystery.

The evening song was especially meaningful as Brenton sang it as a Helper for the first time. He smiled at Verdie and put his arm around her as they sang the last verse together:

> *And so we hope, when night is come*
> *That you have found your way back home*
> *To fire and warmth, to kin and friend,*
> *To love and joy at journey's end*

He had found love and joy, but it was not at journeys end; he had found it on the path, in spite of the hardships along the way. He thought about his journey, and realized that it was not over; he had received Meyer's name, and he needed to find him. He also wanted to see Father Bayle one more time; he had told no one of this but Verdie.

It was raining when Brenton woke the next morning. Joe was already up and out of the tent, so Brenton rose and dressed, slipping on his shoes and jacket. He found Verdie in the shelter with Joe and Natia, waiting for him to wake before going to the pool. The urgency that he had felt before was gone, and he enjoyed the walk in spite of the misty rain. The water was cool and refreshing and tasted better than it had before. He was healed now, and this source was no longer critical to him, but it felt life-giving nonetheless. He felt compelled to fill a flask before rising from the Kneeling Stone.

Carwyn and Uncle Lloyd were seated with the four friends for the morning meal, and the talk turned to the future. Joe was eager to get an invitation to Mark. He had been thinking like a Helper for a long time in spite of the disease, and his hopes for healing had not been just for himself, but also for his friends. Brenton spoke of Meyer's invitation, and then he brought up the subject that had haunted his thoughts since he had learned of his parent's murder.

"I want to talk to Father Bayle," he said bluntly.

Verdie looked at him, remembering their talk at the Close.

Carwyn and Uncle Lloyd stopped what they were doing.

"You know that he is dangerous, yes?" asked Carwyn.

"I have no fear of him," replied Brenton, "and I want to ask him about my parents."

Uncle Lloyd was slow to speak.

"I have seen him several times since I buried your parents, and he has never spoken to me. If you go, you must use caution. Your lack of fear may serve you well, or it may betray you."

Brenton nodded, determined to go.

Joe wanted to go with his friend, but Natia expressed fear for his safety so he decided to stay with her. Verdie wanted to speak up, but deep inside she knew that Brenton needed to face Father Bayle. She offered support, but Brenton didn't want her to go anywhere near Father Bayle, even if she were to stay outside the Village. Carwyn volunteered to escort Brenton, and he offered the services of his companions, Umit and Constant. It was agreed that they would leave later that day for the campsite across the lake, up the eastern road.

After the meal cleanup, Carwyn pulled Brenton aside.

"We have a ceremony to complete before we travel," he said. "Come with me."

Verdie knew what was coming, and she smiled as she followed Brenton to a small table under a broad oak near the shelter. Umit and Constant were there, and Uncle Lloyd sat at the table with his back to the tree. Carwyn beckoned Joe and Natia to watch, and soon they were all standing around the table as Brenton was seated. Cara and Leila saw the ceremony taking shape and joined to watch.

"This is tradition," Uncle Lloyd began. "I was very happy to write your name and Joe's on the hands of these lovely warriors," he said looking up at Cara and her companions with a fatherly smile. "Now I am honored to write Meyer's name on your hand, and I hope to see the day that he is healed." Uncle Lloyd was holding a pen, and he dipped it in an inkwell. "Hold out your hands, Brenton."

Brenton complied, and soon Uncle Lloyd was scrawling the names in bold black letters on the back of Brenton's hands.

"Do you know why we do this?" Uncle Lloyd asked gravely.

"Yes, it is a reminder of our duty," Brenton said, remembering Natia's words that morning not long ago in the grassy hollow.

Everyone looked at him and smiled.

Uncle Lloyd marked the other three in the party. Joe's invitation to Mark would go with them to the Village, along with one for Mr. Parish. The names were covered in fluid from Azure Succuro stems, fixing the ink in place. After the ceremony, Verdie and Natia helped Joe and

Brenton prepare invitations for their friends, taking the time to show them time-honored traditions in the print and graphics. When the invitations were dried and stowed, Verdie and Brenton spent the rest of the morning talking about Brenton's trip and the training that he would undergo in order to help others climb The Mountain.

After the noon meal, Verdie helped Brenton with final preparations. His new traveling companions were waiting for him by the shelter when they emerged from the tent, Brenton proudly wearing his father's jacket, its very presence with him now refreshing his vision at the Fall and his future with Verdie. Joe and Natia appeared, as did Cara and Leila.

Uncle Lloyd had some final advice for Brenton.

"Do not attempt to challenge Father Bayle." Brenton listened with respect to his wise elder. "He and those around him are too powerful for us to confront. If he fell, another would rise in his place. Our task is to help others climb The Mountain, not to try to overtake the Flatlands or its Villages by force. Our calling leads us on another path."

Brenton thought of the Climbers and their protests at Mt. Nabal. Then he remembered his vision at the Fall. He had not shared it with anyone, and hearing Uncle Lloyd warn him about unseating Father Bayle made him wonder what his future might hold.

The travelers said their goodbyes and set off down the eastward path. Brenton was glad to be in full control of his faculties as he lowered himself down First Climb. On the beach, Dale and Trent were fishing as they often did, but were prepared to hawk their wares to any Newcomers in spite of the gloomy weather.

The Helpers stripped and crossed Lake Yarden without incident, and on the far bank Carwyn asked them to help him dismantle the small corral where the old horses had been kept. The cart had not returned, but Carwyn wanted to make a permanent end of Elder Younger's practice of selling water from the fall on the beach to the Nutrition Bureau.

Brenton thought of what the disruption might mean to Father Bayle and the Ascending Day ceremony. He discussed this with the other Helpers as they worked, and there was no small amount of humor in the conversation.

They finished their work and made their way east, camping again in the enclosure by the shallow cave at the base of the rock wall. The next morning they moved on quietly under sullen skies. Birds became more scarce as they traveled east, and the land became more barren. Brenton realized how quickly the foliage at The Mountain had come to seem normal, and he thought of the dry gardens in the Village, and the pitiful pots on Mt. Nabal. At the intersection with the north and south road, the small band of Helpers went straight east, into the Flatlands. Brenton remembered Cara's words about alternatives to the road, and asked Carwyn if he knew the way through the wilderness.

"All you have to do is follow," Carwyn replied. "There is a place you must see."

By noon they were deep into the Flatlands. They had passed to the north of Fortress Rock, and the hill with the plateau where Brenton and his friends had first encountered the men with weapons. The Helpers kept a steady, brisk pace, and Brenton was ready for a break. He mentioned this to Constant, who was walking directly in front of him.

"Just a little farther and we will stop," he said reassuringly.

Brenton kept going although by now his legs were begging him to slow down. They hadn't gone much farther when Carwyn angled northeast. They climbed a low rise, and when they had reached the summit they were overlooking a shallow little bowl-shaped valley with several unnatural piles of rock at its lowest point. Carwyn took off his pack and the others followed. Carwyn was reverent as he spoke.

"Brenton, Uncle Lloyd told you that one day a friend would take you to the place where your parents lie. I am that friend, and today we have arrived at this hallowed place." He pointed down the incline to the rocks. "We do not recall who lies beneath which stones, but we Helpers come here often to reflect on our duty."

Brenton looked at the names printed on his hands, then back at the mounds in the little valley.

The others seated themselves on rocks and prepared to eat as Brenton descended the incline. He knelt in the middle of the mounds and turned in a circle on his knees, paying his respect to each grave. He was overcome with sadness as memories of his mother and father flooded his thoughts, seeing them clearly now, their loving faces and pleasant voices indelibly printed on his mind. His dreams of them had been memories. Sadness was replaced by a peaceful feeling, knowing that they had died seeking healing. They wanted healing for him, too, and now their hopes for him had been fulfilled. He took strength from the place for what lay ahead.

He stayed a while, and the faces of his parent's friends began to appear; he remembered calling them "Aunt" and "Uncle," an endearing term that made them all feel like family. His healed mind held much he could not yet see.

Eventually he joined the others to eat, and he drank refreshing water from The Fall from his flask. That gave him an idea, and Carwyn, watching him and discerning the idea as it formed, nodded his approval. Before they left, Brenton poured a little healing water on each grave.

They moved on, and Carwyn had one more sight for Brenton to see. At mid afternoon they came to a very flat area with no rock outcroppings and very few trees and grasses. As they walked across it Carwyn pointed Brenton to the northern edge. The Helpers waited for him as he walked in the direction that Carwyn indicated, and he didn't know what he was looking for, but soon he noticed stones nearly flush with the ground, organized in connected rectangles. He walked around the stone rectangles for a moment and then paused as it struck him: it was an old foundation, and erosion had exposed the once-buried stones.

Verdie had said that the Flatlands had once been green and inhabited, and he turned, looking back at The Mountain. Although the land around him was brown, The Mountain looked exactly as it had in his vision at the Fall. He contemplated what it could mean and then rejoined the others and they continued east. Brenton asked many questions that afternoon to which few answers were given. Brenton was reminded more than once that over time he would learn many things.

Late in the day, in fading light, they reached the grassy hollow where Brenton had first met Helpers; Umit took the first watch. By now word of Mr. Astor's demise and the failure of his mission would have reached the Village.

Less than a day's walk east, Father Bayle sat at his expansive dining table with Yap, leash and all, perched comfortably in his lap. He poured clear water into an ornate goblet and began drumming his groomed nails on the exotic wood, waiting for the man in the forest-green jacket to return.

22. In the Apartments of Father Bayle

The next morning, as the small band walked the final distance to the Village, Brenton mulled over what he might say; he didn't yet have a plan for confronting Father Bayle about his parents. Mt. Nabal was growing on the horizon as he imagined sitting in the stuffy little office where Father Bayle met Villagers to give an impression of his deprivation and humility, very few of them having seen inside his expansive apartments. He wondered if Father Bayle would try to harm him, but even that thought no longer held fear.

The closer they came to Nabal, the quieter the group became. Brenton had been lost in thought for some time, while the others simply did not like the Village and had little to talk about. Brenton walked beside Carwyn to plan how the group would support him.

They agreed that he should wait until early evening before going into the Village, and then the others would follow one by one. He was to go into the Mountain Club and seek out Father Bayle while the others took up positions nearby. Brenton did not know if he would find Father Bayle there, or how long he might stay in the building, but Carwyn reassured him that the group would be vigilant: if Carwyn felt that too much time had passed, he and the others would intervene. Once Brenton had his satisfaction at the outcome of the conversation, the group would use the cover of darkness to seek out three houses and leave invitations.

It was a comfort to know that he would have friends nearby, but that didn't solve the problem of what Brenton would say to his former benefactor. Brenton considered how he and his friends had been like puppets on a stage, and Brenton would at least have the possibility of finding out how big that stage might be.

The Helpers were in no hurry, and they arrived near their goal by mid-afternoon. Waiting for darkness, they stayed out of sight among rocks just off the rise to the Village. As he waited, Brenton thought about this place that he had called home his whole life, and which now felt foreign to him. At the Helper camp he'd had everything he needed, and didn't miss anything left behind in his little house; he wondered briefly what would become of the little cottage on Leeway Street.

Darkness came early under a heavy cloud-laden sky. Brenton pulled on a grey cloak to cover his jacket, and before hoisting his pack, checked the contents. He made sure that, among other things, he had the three invitations and the flask from the pool. He took some final instruction and encouragement, and then he was off up the last rise to the gate, taking the same path that another Helper had taken not long before. Verdie had told him that Cara shadowed the friends in the Flatlands the night he left Nabal, leaving him wondering what assignments he might be given in the future.

He reached the Village gate, pulled up the grey hood, and eased the portal open without creaking, just enough to squeeze through. He made his way north and east toward the center of town, the dark streets that had aided others following him now aiding his mission. He passed several Villagers along the way, but they took no notice of him. He was nervous but unafraid as he approached Mt. Nabal near the wagon gate. He walked around it to the entrance and slipped unnoticed into the foyer. He paused for a moment, listening to the activity in the kitchen, but did not hear anything that sounded like Father Bayle or Yap, so he entered the auditorium, making his way with deliberate steps to the office door.

He removed his hood and paused, thinking of Verdie, picturing her face and her wind-swept blonde hair, and a picture of his father wearing the green jacket came to him. Those images gave him all the resolve that he needed, and he reached up and knocked on the door with a firm but respectful rap. He heard the sounds he hoped for: Yap immediately began his noise making, and that soon mingled with the clicking of Father Bayle's boots. The lock clicked, the handle moved, the door opened, and there in the little, stuffy office stood the tall man in the crimson robe holding a little ball of fur.

Father Bayle smiled broadly.

"Brenton!!" he exclaimed over the yapping, "You've come back to us!"

"Well, not exa..."

"Come in! Come in, by all means," Father Bayle interrupted, as he gestured broadly, stepping out of the doorway, head tilted slightly.

"Well...thank you," Brenton managed.

"We've missed you. We've been speculating on when you might return, and now here you are!" Father Bayle was behind Brenton now.

"I am back, but not to stay," Brenton said as Father Bayle passed him and opened the door to the parlor, gesturing Brenton in.

"Oh, really?" Father Bayle's tone was exaggerated. "Where are you staying now?"

He knows what a Helper's cloak and shoes look like, Brenton thought to himself. But what he said was, "Joe and I went to visit Verdie. We have made some new friends and we have decided to stay with them."

Father Bayle's eyes closed as his brows arched, his lower lip protruding.

"Humph," he grunted. "Are you quite sure? You know that your friends both came back from their foray into the wild lands."

So it is confirmed, thought Brenton, *Meyer is here.*

"Well, yes, I knew that," Brenton lied. "I have made up my mind, really, and I have come back to speak with you and ask you some questions."

Brenton followed Father Bayle as he made his way to the office in his apartments. His crimson robe fluttered as he walked, and he was still holding Yap, who was quiet now.

"Well, questions can wait. First we must have a drink."

They were in a large, opulent office, and Father Bayle gestured him to a seat and lowered the dog to the floor, clipping the leash to a metal ring affixed to the desk.

"How is my dear Verdie?" he asked, trying to sound fatherly, fumbling in a cupboard.

"Oh, she is quite well...yes quite, " but what he wanted to say was, *She never wants to see you again.* "She is very happy where she is now." Knowing full well that Father Bayle knew where she was, Brenton avoided saying "The Mountain," unsure of the reaction.

Father Bayle found what he was looking for: two cups and a tall, blue bottle.

"Well, I am very glad to hear that," he said, as he set cups down and began to pour. "What about your house, your job? I'm concerned that you may be making a very poor decision."

Brenton was about to reply when Father Bayle continued.

"And what about your Preservation Reward? Surely that must be important to you!" Father Bayle sat across from him, indicating the cups. "Drink! Please!" He said, smiling, and Brenton didn't hesitate.

Father Bayle put the tips of his fingers together, palms apart, grinning coldly as Brenton drained the cup and asked for more. It tasted foul, but that didn't stop him.

"Oh, yes, yes of course!" Father Bayle was smiling broadly, and he was being the perfect host as he poured another cup, staring intently at Brenton.

As Brenton had readied to leave their hiding place, Carwyn had given him valuable information. Having been healed, drugged water would no longer affect him, because it worked with the disease that he no longer carried.

Brenton was tempted to act as though he were succumbing to the water, but then, laughing to himself, decided not to. It would be more fun to see Father Bayle squirm, and he didn't wait long.

"So...you've been...you've been traveling? When...uh...When did you arrive?"

Father Bayle fidgeted nervously as Brenton smiled across the desk at him, asking for more water, enjoying himself immensely.

"Yes, I have been traveling. I arrived earlier this evening," he said, as Father Bayle rose and crossed the room, shutting the door.

"Traveling alone?" Father Bayle wanted to know, as the door slammed shut.

Brenton was still unafraid, and rose.

"No, I have been on the road with some new friends," and as he said this he quickly removed the cloak, revealing the forest-green jacket. He was looking at Father Bayle who was making his way back to his seat when the cloak came off, the sight freezing him mid-stride. Brenton looked down at his coat, then back at Father Bayle. "Oh, Joe has one of these, too. And Verdie. And Meyer got one, and I have one for Mark."

Father Bayle tried to return to his seat casually.

"Very nice, very nice," he said nervously, trying to figure out what to say next, as Brenton sat down.

"Let us get to why I am here, if you please."

Father Bayle didn't say anything. He was seated with fist to chin, elbow resting on the arm of the chair, staring at Brenton when he gestured for him to proceed. Realizing that he would not be able to use his regular techniques, he was busily working out a plan.

Brenton started out slowly.

"Do you know what happened...," Brenton began, then paused, baiting Father Bayle.

"Happened to what?" Father Bayle was becoming irritated.

"What happened to my storybooks? I had them when I first moved here."

His dream of Father Bayle in his room, pouring water and taking his books, was a memory.

"There were no books. The only books in Nabal are mine, and the ones I give to the school." At this he smiled and paused. "You came here destitute and alone after your parents died at the Health Bureau."

"Are you sure? I am sure that I had them in my room." Brenton was ready to push harder as Father Bayle squirmed a little, but the older man was still confident in his superiority, both mentally and physically.

"No, I'm quite sure," Father Bayle said, smiling again.

"I am quite certain that I saw you come into my room and take them, leaving me some water from a tall, blue bottle in their place." Now it was Brenton smiling as he indicated the bottle.

"Is that what you came for? Books?" Father Bayle realized that the game was up, his voice rose, and a twinge of anger that Brenton had never heard before stained his words.

"That is one thing I came for. I know that you have them. But there is something else, something Uncle Lloyd told me," and at that Father Bayle stiffened, but said nothing. "I visited a curious place in the Flatlands just yesterday. It was a little valley with ten stone piles."

Father Bayle paused before saying, "And what were you told?" His voice was cold and low.

"You know what I was told. My parents are buried there with the parents of my friends. I came to find out your part in their deaths."

Father Bayle had been trying to act his normal gregarious self when Brenton arrived, opting for his usual trick of drugged water, but now he was flustered because it had not worked, and he couldn't understand why. He didn't want to resort to violence, but he started to think he might have to. But just then an idea struck, and he changed the subject completely.

"Meyer came back to the Village a few days ago." Father Bayle was smiling, looking comfortable as he reviewed manicured fingernails. Brenton was momentarily distracted by the deflection, but caught himself; of course Father Bayle wasn't going to implicate himself in the murder of ten innocent people.

"Yes, I know," said Brenton, trying to work the conversation back to his purpose. "I asked you what part you had in my parent's death."

"Meyer told me all about your little adventure on the beach," Father Bayle was smiling broadly, speaking slowly and annunciating meticulously.

That caught Brenton completely off guard. *How would Meyer know about that?* he wondered.

"I am asking you about my parents," Brenton insisted firmly, trying to put questions about Meyer out of mind.

"The poor boy. He rode in on a wagon and came straight to me."

He rode in on a wagon? The Nutrition Bureau tried to stop him just days ago. Brenton was succumbing and becoming confused.

"Bayle, I am asking if you had anything to do with the death of ten innocent people." Brenton had never called him "Bayle" before. It was Brenton who was flustered now. Bayle sensed it and grinned, adding to Brenton's mounting frustration. Brenton felt that something bad was about to happen, and he tried to think of Verdie.

"He told me he was sorry." Bayle paused for effect. "I didn't really believe him." Bayle was cool, his demeanor beginning to drive the younger man mad; Brenton was losing control.

"Sorry for what?" he blurted out.

Bayle had Brenton right where he wanted him.

"Oh...he said he was sorry for going along with the plan that I put in place with Elder Younger, but I think he meant to all along." Bayle's demeanor was oozing honey, his words dripping blue poison.

Brenton's healed mind recalled that night on the Grand Resting Plane, and the anger that had been rising toward Bayle shifted to Meyer. *It was deliberate! Meyer had known all along,* he thought. He had almost been murdered, and Meyer had been complicit in the plot. Again! Brenton's mind was racing, and he felt doubly justified for not forgiving Meyer. Healed though he was in body, his mind grasped at the selfishness it had once coddled, and he swore revenge, livid with Meyer and his treachery!

Father Bayle was sitting across the desk from him, grinning from ear to ear, shadowy crow's-feet fanning back from wrinkle-rimmed eyes across stretched cheeks. Yap lay contentedly by the desk, curled in a little ball, oblivious to the coiling tension.

Brenton sat still, trying to collect himself, struggling to set anger for Meyer aside. He had to deal with Bayle once and for all. Meyer could be dealt with later.

Finally, his healed mind allowed him to gather his feelings and compartmentalize his anger. Looking intently at Bayle who was still grinning, Brenton said through clenched teeth,

"You have not answered my question. Were you responsible for the death of my parents?"

He was seething at both Bayle and Meyer, but in this moment he tried to concentrate on Bayle.

Bayle realized that his attempt at diversion had failed. In spite of his obvious anger which Bayle had studied on faces for a very long time, Brenton was still insistent on his question, and now a denial of accusations would not suffice.

Bayle knew all about the little valley in the Flatlands; it was he who had the adults poisoned. He had taken the children by force and tried to erase their memories, thinking for a long time that he had succeeded, until Verdie left. He had always regretted not making Cara disappear, too.

Now there was just one thing to do, and he could say anything that came to mind because his victim would never escape.

"I'll answer your questions!" Anger was rising as Bayle stood, leaning ominously across the desk. Brenton had never seen him angry.

"You are the son of a rebellious, filthy peasant! I do not tolerate rebels, and I hate you peasants. I use the means at my disposal to protect the Village!" He was gesturing with his arm and finger in the air, his voice rising in self-righteous indignation, and he wasn't done. "You know nothing of the history of this Village—MY VILLAGE!!" If ever he was challenged, which rarely happened, he used the protection of "the Village" as justification to do anything he chose to do, or to coerce others to do his bidding.

Brenton slowly rose, anger rising at the characterization of his father. He was not going to let Bayle intimidate him.

"Just tell me what you did to my parents," he said coolly.

Now Bayle was the one becoming enraged, intolerant as he was of insolence. The last person who had stood up to him was wearing the same jacket that now glared across the desk, the memory of it infuriating him, having long thought that he had eliminated a threat to his power. He fixed his gaze on Brenton, and then drew back, clasped hands behind him, stepped sideways, and began to move around the desk. As he did, he slid a hand out and grasped a small vial.

"As I said," he was trying to calm his voice, but he was not successful. "I do not tolerate REBELS!"

His face was beet-red now, and as he yelled "rebels" he leapt forward, catching Brenton off guard. Bayle was a tall man, and strong. He hit Brenton at the shoulders and his momentum knocked Brenton backwards, Bayle crashing down on top of him, pinning arms to chest.

"Now you'll get what your father got!" Bayle was livid.

He used a forearm to pin his former charge's neck to the floor as he fumbled with the vial. Brenton squirmed, trying to free himself, but the weight of the murderous man held him fast. The vial was open, and

Bayle tried to force it on Brenton whose mouth was shut, head shaking wildly back and forth, the memory of Mr. Astor's vial fresh.

Brenton had difficulty breathing, and while trying to steal a breath, Bayle succeeded. Brenton tasted the horrible liquid, eyes wide, gasping for air. Bayle held fast, waiting for the poison to work. Brenton tried to spit, but he swallowed involuntarily; Bayle saw it and smiled. "That should do it," he said grinning, his hot breath a stench.

Bayle had been experimenting for years and had become an accomplished chemist. He used Azure Succuro root—the petals and stems of which the Helpers used for healing—to develop drugs by using the mind-altering substances in various ways. A small amount in the water supply was enough to keep the population under control and dizzy if they tried to climb anything above a stair. A little more on Ascending Days increased the euphoria while insuring his dominance, and eased the imposed dizziness. A variation in the tall blue bottle worked on memory and allowed him to suggest ideas to a victim while masking others. Mr. Astor had used a version that induced terror and amplification of the awareness and symptoms of the Flatlander's disease. The concoction that Brenton had just ingested was Bayle's pride and joy, used only on special occasions, and with only one outcome.

Brenton choked on the insidious fluid which tasted worse than whatever Mr. Astor had forced on him. He was pinned under the weight of Bayle, the wild-eyed face just inches from his own, obnoxious breath delivered in even, disgusting doses. He could feel the overpowering strength of his former mentor. Brenton lost hope and stopped squirming.

It was then that he felt the effects of the drug. It didn't touch his mind as the other had; this went to muscles. He was surprised to palpably feel strength building, muscles tensing, his mind registering power rising, and he let it build. Suddenly, and without giving any sign, he arched his back and pushed with all his new might, and Bayle was off him.

Brenton leapt up, feeling strong as ever. He looked at Bayle as the confused man scrambled to his feet, crimson robes tangling. In the scuffle his high crimson collar came loose, and now his strained, tangled robes pulled back at the neck, revealing a large, red tattoo.

"What you...intended...for harm...has turned out... for good," Brenton said, panting and smiling, confidence building.

Bayle was shocked but regained his footing. He crouched facing Brenton, arms out to his sides. His back was to a tall shelf, Brenton's to the room. Bayle stared at him, then at the vial. He dared to touch a drop to his tongue, then spat, trying to understand why the drug had had a reverse effect.

Brenton saw Bayle off guard and rushed him with all the power he could muster, crashing into him, slamming him against the shelf, arms out to his sides, Bayle's hand still grasping the vial. A little brown box tumbled to the floor and with it, storybooks. Brenton backed away, leaving Bayle against the shelf, a horrified look on his face, his wide-eyed gaze transfixed on the box, his arms unmoved.

Brenton recognized his books and looked at the oddly familiar yet out of place little box, dingy and dusty as it was. He stooped to pick it up and held it, looking at Bayle, whose eyes followed it.

Brenton opened the lid and was startled by a flight of large black moths rushing from captivity. He looked inside and there he saw a corrupted, moth-eaten pair of once beautiful shoes, a few decorative silver studs still surrounding what remained of a triad of pickaxes on the top. Brenton slowly raised his gaze to Bayle whose stare was affixed to the box, a look of desperate horror etched on his face.

For all of his pomp and ceremony, his freedom about the Village, his gregarious mannerisms, his apparent good deeds and his false benevolence, Brenton realized that the pitiful figure in front of him was the one who was trapped, and it was he who was free. The disease that was worse than the one he had once carried would never let go of the mind of Father Bayle.

Brenton dropped the box on the floor, picked up his stolen books, snatched the vile from a frozen hand, and, taking his cloak off the chair, turned to go. Yap managed to pull his leash free from the desk and followed him quietly out the office door and into the parlor. Brenton let himself out of the office, through the auditorium and out into the night, pulling his cloak and hood on and stowing vial and books. He had faced Bayle. Now he had business with Meyer.

Back in the office, the awkwardly frozen Bayle was still leaning back against the shelf, the bitter taste of his own drug still in his mouth, his mind replaying long-repressed scenes. It had been a very, very long time since Bayle's mind had dredged up the memory of that day so long ago, and now he had no control over it. He had stood in the water behind the Fall on Chasm's Close, uninvited, stolen shoes still on, when the vision came.

Now his heart slowly beat to the rhythm of a sledgehammer as the handsome man in the forest-green jacket, with insignia on the arms and over the heart, relentlessly pounded the Water Dispensary. The woman at his side, her short, blonde, wind-swept hair bouncing with every thud, kept time with a hammer of her own.

23. Written On His Hands

Brenton headed for Meyer's house, not waiting for Carwyn and the others to emerge from shadow. Mr. Parish's house was closer but that could wait. The strength that Brenton felt matched the anger at Meyer that he had repressed, and now it came to the fore. Meyer had deliberately betrayed him and then pretended to alert Verdie to cover his deception. Brenton had come close to death both on the beach and on The Mountain. *Meyer will pay for this*, he determined, uncertain exactly what he would do, his thoughts blood-red with vengeance.

The other Helpers watched from concealment as he left the Mountain Club. They eventually caught up with him, walking briskly. They could not see his face, and Carwyn wondered at his pace.

"Did you find Father Bayle?" Carwyn wanted to know.

"Yes," Brenton replied through clenched teeth.

"What was the outcome of the meeting?"

Brenton's old selfishness welled as he replied. "Later," he said as he marched.

"To which house are we going?"

Brenton usually had the questions. "Meyer's," he snapped.

Carwyn exchanged glances with Umit and Constant, puzzled at Brenton's tone; Carwyn was worried.

The questions stopped and they walked to Meyer's house in tense silence. Arriving at the fence, Brenton told the others he needed to see Meyer alone. Carwyn insisted that Brenton put the invitation at the entry, but Brenton was determined, climbed the fence, and then climbed over the railing on to the darkened porch. The others stayed in shadow as Brenton knocked.

"Who is it?" a sluggish, suspicious voice asked.

"An old friend," Brenton replied, his voice low and menacing.

One after the other the locks turned, and the door opened a crack. It was all the invitation he needed, and Brenton pushed inside. A startled Meyer backed away, nearly fainting when the grey hood came off.

"Hello, Meyer," Brenton snarled, his face etched with anger, red from the exertion of his fight and pace.

Meyer cowered, his drugged mind remembering bits and snatches of what he had done to his friend.

Brenton knew that Meyer would be drugged and that he might not remember much of what he had done, so he took out the flask from the camp pool, and just as he had done near Fortress Rock, he shoved the flask in Meyer's face and forced him to drink, wanting Meyer fully alert.

Meyer gasped for air as he choked the water down. His eyes widened with the shock of a cleansed mind, the full recognition of the anger on Brenton's face striking him. Memories only recently masked came flooding back, and he backed away until he hit a wall.

"I didn't mean to hurt you!" he pleaded, overwhelmed and helpless.

Brenton felt no pity for Meyer who had tasted a cure but still chose to cause harm.

"You lied to me!" Brenton yelled at him, taking a step forward.

"I know I did, and I'm sorry!" Meyer was worried for his safety. He had wept bitter tears on the cliffs above the beach when he realized that he might never talk to Brenton again, and now he faced his infuriated friend in his own home.

"Elder Younger drugged me, just like Father Bayle," he said, sinking to his knees, his eyes pleading for mercy.

Brenton took another step, standing menacingly over him.

"You almost got me killed!" He blurted out. His face turned a shade redder as he added with a shout in Meyer's face, "THREE TIMES!"

He was out of control, remembering how close he had come to death, and in that state his mind reverted to self-preservation. He wanted to strike.

Meyer, on his knees, lowered head in hands and wept as he had above the beach, truly sorry.

Brenton looked down, unmoved. "Look at me, Meyer!" He was not going to hit Meyer with head down.

Meyer looked, pleading eyes red, cheeks dripping tears.

"I'm sorry Brenton, really sorry. Please, won't you forgive me?"

Brenton grabbed Meyer's collar with is left hand, and raised his right in a fist to strike. As he did this, he exposed the back of both hands; they both saw the names written there at the same time.

Meyer was stunned. He had not noticed the tradition of the Helpers in his time around them, and he didn't know what his name on Brenton's hand meant, but he could see it meant something to Brenton.

Brenton froze, staring at Meyer's name on his hand, images suddenly flooding his healed mind: the Close and Meyer's name etched in his mind behind the plume at The Fall, Uncle Lloyd printing on his hand and asking about the meaning, Natia's face as she had told him what it meant in the hollow, and finally a smiling Verdie standing on the beach.

He looked at the pleading face as Meyer mouthed, "Please forgive me."

With a sudden gratefulness for complete healing, a wave of emotion swept over Brenton. Looking into Meyer's face now he realized that

Meyer had been a victim, and that he *was* truly sorry. Bayle had lied in a ploy to anger him, and it had almost worked. If he were to remain truly free, the changes that he had chosen would have to control him, not the past. Brenton had the chance—and the duty—to offer Meyer real freedom in the act of forgiveness, but instead Brenton was about to strike him.

Brenton lowered his fist and let Meyer's collar slip out of his grasp. He was the one who needed forgiveness. He slowly lowered himself to his knees, the anger rushing out, sorrow over what he had nearly done overcoming him. He was free of the disease, free of Bayle, and now he was free to forgive; it was the fulfillment of his duty, the way that he had chosen.

He looked at his hands and then at Meyer with his red eyes and tear-stained face. Compassion for his friend welled up, and he understood how much Meyer needed his forgiveness and healing. He hugged Meyer, sobbing, imagining him drinking pure water at The Fall on the Close.

"I forgive you, Meyer," he said through his tears, his head still buried in his friends shoulder. "I forgive you for everything."

Meyer had watched the transformation in his friend's face, and now he was receiving the forgiveness that his clear mind had longed for. As Brenton released Meyer from the past, self-pity that had rooted withered in the embrace, and the weight of Brenton's forgiveness brought tears of joy.

The other Helpers had come into the house unnoticed just before Brenton raised his fist, and they watched the friends embrace.

The tears ended and the friends rose, Brenton turning to see the other three Helpers in the room smiling at him.

"Your true healing has begun in earnest," Carwyn said with a confident smile.

Brenton smiled back at him. Then he looked at Meyer, remembering his mission and his duty.

"I have something for you," he told Meyer as he retrieved his things. He fumbled in the pack, removing the invitations, selecting one for Meyer and handing it to him.

Meyer wiped away tears as he tried to comprehend the package.

The realization of what he held suddenly overcame him. He struggled with the string, so Brenton helped him open it. Meyer read aloud:

> The real you sense
> Is surely not
> The real that Real
> Can be
> If you would taste
> The really Real
> I urge you, Climb with me!

He looked at Brenton and smiled, and Brenton indicated that he should turn the invitation over. Written there was the one thing that Meyer had longed for:

You belong!

Brenton

Meyer was ecstatic. He hugged Brenton, then he hugged the other Helpers, and this time it wasn't awkward the way it had been in the Flatlands at the cave.

Brenton pulled a forest-green jacket from his pack and handed it to Meyer.

"Wear it with pride," Brenton told him, and Meyer, quickly pulling it on, said that he would.

"I have one more thing for you, Meyer," Brenton said softly, pulling a little brown box from his pack.

Epilogue: The Mountain

What followed in Nabal would have a profound effect on everyone who lived there. Things would never be the same for the people of the Village, and the life of Horatio Fenwick Bayle (for that was his given name) was about to change dramatically.

Brenton and Joe took training on leading the climb, and they often climbed with others to the Close. Each time he went, Brenton lingered on the headwall, looking over the Close, but his eyes were always drawn to the distant mountains away to the southwest. He remembered Leila emerging from The Fall the day he was healed. Her mention of her homeland beyond those mountains lingered in his memory and drew his thoughts southward.

Duck responded to his invitation from Verdie, and she delighted in helping him climb. He received his healing with the innocence of a child and she cried for joy with him, just as she had with Brenton.

How Duck broke away from the influence of Elder Younger, and indeed what happened to Elder Younger, is a story reserved for Helper campfires. The same should be said about Meyer, Mark, and Mr. Parish's experiences.

Uncle Lloyd set some time aside with Brenton to tell him about his last vision under The Fall. It seemed that Brenton's father carried with him a package that only Brenton could open, and before he died he asked Uncle Lloyd to send it off, away from The Mountain, for safekeeping. His father hoped that one day Brenton would come to The Mountain and retrieve the package. The vision had reminded the old man of it, and he had instructions for Brenton.

For his part Brenton had questions about Father Bayle, the mystery of the moth-eaten shoes, and the origin of the storybooks. Uncle Lloyd told him many things that stirred his imagination and curiosity, but even Uncle Lloyd was not able to provide all of the answers that Brenton craved.

Helpers patrolling the Flatlands reported that the little valley with the ten stone mounds had become filled with Azure Succuro, the brightest and most beautiful of the blooms growing out of the rock mounds themselves. Pouring healing water from The Fall over the graves of the departed became a solemn Helper tradition.

More and more villagers began arriving from Nabal as more and more names were being whispered behind the plume at The Fall. The road west became much more dangerous, corresponding with the Nutrition Bureau undergoing some leadership changes. Patrols of Helpers were sent out into the Flatlands regularly, Brenton and Joe among them.

During one patrol, a large number of men in field-grey uniforms were seen moving north along the road at the western edge of the ranch, heading toward the Nutrition Bureau. A giant of a man, bald with gold earrings and with two ferocious animals straining on chain leashes, kept cadence in the lead. He was later seen heading east toward Nabal accompanied by his beasts.

The day finally came for Brenton to lead a climb. He and Verdie assembled their party after the morning meal, and all were eager to go.

Brenton broke away from the group and picked some Azure Succuro. Verdie was watching him, and he beckoned her a little ways up the path. They knelt in the lush grass near some grave markers, Brenton taking a moment to reflect on his mission as a Helper. Their thoughts were united in reverence for those who had gone before, hope for their journey, and joy at the prospect of climbing together.

After a brief moment together they rose, and looking over the Newcomers, Brenton was overwhelmed with delight at the chance to lead his first climb. He would never tire of seeing Newcomers arrive at the Fall for the first time, to drink true healing. The very thought of sharing the experience drove his desire to climb, and he felt love for these new climbing companions. He thought about what he could say to instill hope in the group.

"This is a great day," he began, smiling, although his tone was serious. "You have all come here freely. Each of you brings your experiences from the Flatlands or the Climbers Village, whatever they may be. You bring your doubts and fears and your uncertainty about the path ahead. Most importantly you bring a determination to climb to the Fall on Chasm's Close, in the belief that you can be truly healed. I cannot tell you what you will experience; that is for you to discover. I can only tell you what I have learned by going there myself, and I am eager to return."

Turning his gaze toward the heights and smiling broadly, he blurted out in what sounded almost like a song,

"The Mountain is steep and rough and treacherous but, climbing together, I assure you, there will be joy in the journey!"

He turned and, taking Verdie's hand, they took to the path. The Newcomers looked at each other, then up at The Mountain. The encouraging words of the leader's promise rang in their ears. Fear melted away in the warmth of the sun, and belief rose in them as smiles illuminated faces.

With an outstretched arm pointing up The Mountain, Brenton shouted joyfully over his shoulder,

"To the Upper Reaches, the Fall on Chasm's Close, and the possibility of complete healing!"

He breathed in the cool open air of the late summer morning and began walking west toward the trailhead. At last, he was free.

About the Author

Steve's formative experiences—combined with a love of a great story—led him to writing. Born and raised in Africa, his early years were spent in boarding school in the rural, Great Lakes region of the Congo. Strict rules competed with freewheeling boyhood adventures to feed a creative, curious mind and established ideas about authority and the world.

There was plenty to fuel the imagination: gunfire in the streets of Kisangani, evacuation by Belgian and American mercenaries from Kinshasa, days-long trips through the rainforest by Land Rover, a boat trip on the Nile complete with 20-ft crocs and giant hippos, seeing (and eating) animals of all types, hunting birds of every description, learning two African languages—young Steve had plenty to ponder.

Later, in a new Pacific Northwest landscape, Steve studied architecture, explored spiritual frontiers, and helped build a family while working in software startups and marketing agencies. This continued to provide fertile ground for deep thinking about the nature of things.

Today, Steve continues to create story worlds, characters, prequels and sequels—and further absorb and appreciate life's gifts.

CPSIA information can be obtained at www.ICGtesting.com
Printed in the USA
BVOW05s1507101014

370135BV00003B/4/P